THE AUTHOR

HOWARD O'HAGAN was born in Lethbridge, Alberta, in 1902. As a young man, he worked on survey parties in the Rockies before moving to Montreal to study law at McGill University. After practising law for a brief time, he returned to western Canada to work as a tour guide in Banff National Park.

Stephen Leacock helped O'Hagan obtain employment with the Canadian Pacific Railroad recruiting farm labourers from England. He also worked for the Canadian National Railroad in Jasper and in New York and for the Argentine National Railroad in Buenos Aires.

While living in San Francisco in the thirties, O'Hagan began a series of sketches of guides, mountain men, and trappers that formed the background for his novel *Tay John* (1939), which he completed on an island in Howe Sound on the British Columbia coast.

One of the first western Canadians to make a major contribution to Canadian literature, O'Hagan found occasional work in the fifties as a journalist in Victoria, British Columbia, and as a labourer on the waterfront and on survey crews.

In 1963 O'Hagan moved to Sicily, where he lived for more than a decade. He returned to Victoria in 1974.

Howard O'Hagan died in Victoria in 1982.

TAY JOHN

HOWARD O'HAGAN

AFTERWORD BY
MICHAEL ONDAATJE

Copyright © 1960, 1974 by Howard O'Hagan
Afterword copyright © 1989 by Michael Ondaatje

First New Canadian Library edition 1989.
This New Canadian Library edition 2008.

First published by Laidlaw and Laidlaw, London, in 1939

Library and Archives Canada Cataloguing in Publication

O'Hagan, Howard, 1902–1982.
    Tay John / Howard O'Hagan ; with an afterword by Michael Ondaatje.

(New Canadian library)
Originally publ.: London : Laidlaw and Laidlaw, 1939.
ISBN 978-0-7710-9392-0

    I. Title. II. Series.

PS8529.H35T39 2008   C813'.54   C2008-900786-7

We acknowledge the financial support of the Government of Canada through the Book Publishing Industry Development Program and that of the Government of Ontario through the Ontario Media Development Corporation's Ontario Book Initiative. We further acknowledge the support of the Canada Council for the Arts and the Ontario Arts Council for our publishing program.

Typeset in Garamond by M&S, Toronto
Printed and bound in Canada

McClelland & Stewart,
a division of Random House of Canada Limited,
a Penguin Random House company
www.penguinrandomhouse.ca

3 4 5   17 16 15

CONTENTS

I am indebted to Mr. Diamond Jenness, of Ottawa, Ontario, for permission to use material appearing in his valuable work, *Indians of Canada*; to Professor Charles Hill-Tout, of Vancouver, B.C., for his advice on the habits of the Salish and Shuswap tribes; and my friends, Jonnie Moyé and Joe Sangré of Fish Lake, near Brulé, Alberta, for many tales of their life and their people.

– Howard O'Hagan

PART ONE

LEGEND

ONE

The time of this in its beginning, in men's time, is 1880 in the summer, and its place is the Athabaska valley, near its head in the mountains, and along the other waters falling into it, and beyond them a bit, over Yellowhead Pass to the westward, where the Fraser, rising in a lake, flows through wilderness and canyon down to the Pacific.

In those days Canada was without a railway across the mountains. The Canadian Pacific was being built, but it was not till 1885 that the first train steamed over its rails to reach tidewater at Port Moody. Its crossing of the Rocky Mountains was by Kicking Horse Pass, more than two hundred miles to the south of Yellowhead. So that it might be built and that men might gain money from its building, Canada was made a dominion. British Columbia, a colony of England, became the most western province of the territory now stretching from the Atlantic to the Pacific.

In time another railway was built. It was called the Grand Trunk Pacific, and passed through the mountains at Yellowhead. That was in 1911.

Until that happened the country around Yellowhead and on the headwaters of the Athabaska, the Arctic's most southern slope, was little changed from what it had always been. It was a game country, and men found meat when they travelled. In the summer the days were long and the nights only brief twilight between the sun's setting and rising. Pine- and fir-trees grew in the valleys, and good grass on the flats and benches; and higher on the mountain slopes, close to the rock and snow, spruce and balsam. Poplar, birch and alder, and tall willows grew in the river bottoms; and everywhere was the sound of running water. In the winters the nights were long. Streams and lakes were frozen. Frost split trees. The wind blew up the Athabaska from the north, and blizzards rose in the valley. Still, sometimes it would be quiet, with the sun shining, and then a man's voice talking could be heard two miles away across the snow.

For a long time fur brigades from Hudson Bay and Fort Garry on the prairies travelled the Athabaska valley. They used horses in the summer and dog-teams in the winter. At first they followed the river to its head, and at the Committee's Punchbowl met those who had come up from the Columbia river valley with beaver skins. For these they exchanged rum and leather and pemmican and came back with the fur eastward. When the lower Columbia valley turned to the Americans and became part of their nation, the brigades swung out of the Athabaska lower down and crossed the mountains at Yellowhead Pass to trade with the Indians and white trappers along the Fraser as far down as Fort Prince George. In time the people around Fort Prince George began to send their furs out by the new Cariboo road to the Pacific, and fur brigades then ceased to travel through the Athabaska valley. The posts they had built in good places where there was

4

game and fish, feed for their horses, and wood for their fires, were no longer used. Their roofs caved in under the snow, and wind blew the moss chinking from between the logs that walled them. Grass grew in the ruts of the trails. Along the trails "blazes," filled with yellow pitch, burned into the tree bark with no one to see them, like lanterns left and forgotten.

In 1880 one man remained by the Athabaska river where it flowed through the mountains. He was tall, fair-haired and fair-bearded, and his blue eyes, stung with the snow, streamed with water when he stood outside and faced the sun. He lived in a cabin on a point above the river where the trail leaves it to follow the Miette to Yellowhead Pass. He trapped and hunted, and traded with bands of wandering Indians. Once a year, in the spring, he took his furs eastward out of the mountains by pack-horse to Edmonton. He was named Red Rorty, and was thought by himself and some others to be a strong man because sometimes on a still day he could be heard shouting from five miles off. He shouted at his horses when they were hard to catch, or at an Indian who had brought poor furs to trade. At other times he would shout when there was nothing to shout for, and would listen and smile when the mountains hurled his voice – rolled it from one rock wall to another, until it seemed he heard bands of men, loosed above him, calling one to another as they climbed farther and higher into the rock and ice.

Much alone, he was given to hearing strange sounds and to seeing a tree far off as a man, or a bunch of trees down the valley from his cabin as a group of men advancing towards him. So that he could see better what was around him and that no one might come upon him unawares, he had made a wide clearing around his cabin, which he kept free of willows and all bush tending to grow there. A pine-tree on the edge of the clearing, ninety yards from his door, was marked with lead from his rifle because of the times in the moonlight he had looked out and thought he saw it moving before him.

His cabin – tidy, with hard earth for its floor – held a stove, a table, a bed, and a bench to sit on. Pack-saddles, bridles, and blankets were hung by its door under the eaves. Its logs were white-washed, so that it gleamed against his eyes from far off when he returned from hunting.

Red Rorty was the first son of many born on a homestead in Bruce County in Ontario. He came west when he was young and worked on the land near Fort Carry. After a while he got a job wrangling horses on a party sent out to the mountains to line the rivers into the contours of the land. When the party disbanded at Edmonton he returned to the Athabaska valley with four horses and the money he had saved, and built himself a cabin – for of all the country he had seen he liked it the best.

When he went into Edmonton with his furs in the spring, or at other times in the autumn, merely because he liked to travel and to have the creak of saddle leather beneath him, he followed other men, who drank and then went down the dirt road, past the church, to the houses in the east-end of the town where the women waited. Then one night he went only as far as the church, held by the singing, and after that passed as much of his time there as he could. It was a new church, different from the others he had known in his earlier days, for its preacher was dressed much as other men, and the members called one another "brother" and "sister." He went to two services on Sunday and to others every night of the week following, because this was a special week in the church.

They sang much and very loudly, and Red Rorty's voice

overtopped all the others. The songs he liked best and remembered so he could sing them to himself when he was afterwards alone, were "Onward, Christian Soldiers," and "Bright With All His Crowns."

After one of the services the minister asked those who so wished to wait and speak to him. Red Rorty waited till the rest had gone and spoke to the minister. They sat in the first row on the hard seats below the pulpit. Their knees touched as they talked.

The minister was a short man and dark-haired. Hair straggled over his pale forehead, and his eyes were half-lidded as he spoke, and looked not at Red Rorty but at the floor beside him. Red Rorty saw mostly the top of his head where the hair was thick and matted as though it had never been combed.

The minister asked what he did and where he came from. Red Rorty told him.

"The world is a big world, my friend, and full of evil." The minister spoke hoarsely, yet low in a whisper, and Red Rorty had to bend closer to hear him. Then:

"Do you believe?" the minister asked after a time.

Red Rorty nodded.

"Do you believe?" the minister asked again, lifting his head and his voice.

"I believe," Red Rorty answered, and the echoes of his voice he thought rolled in the emptied church louder than ever they had in the mountains.

"Do you believe in the Father, the Son and the Holy Ghost?"

"I believe."

"Do you believe that the Son of Man is coming, and that no man knows when He is coming, or where?"

"I believe."

"Do you believe that Jesus Christ, Our Lord, is in all of us and around us, and knows our secret thoughts and sins? That whosoever believeth on Him shall not perish but shall have everlasting life?"

"I believe."

The minister stood up and put his hand on Red Rorty's shoulder.

"We who believe," he said, "are a small army. We must go out and take our message to all the world. By our works we shall be known. You will go back to the mountains. God will show you your work there, and by that work you will be known."

He gave Red Rorty a Bible, and Red Rorty took it back with him to the mountains and read it. He took back with him, too, the preacher's words and the songs sung in the church.

Through the early summer he read the Bible till he knew it well, and could stand with the Book closed and recite chapters to the trees. Of all the words that he read he was most impressed by those that told of Saul of Tarsus, afterwards called Paul, who had left one path of life for another; who went out into the world, among strange people, and preached The Way, and became a great man whose words were remembered.

Then Red Rorty thought that his own life had been sinful, passed in the hope of money and securing food for his belly. It was a life without purpose and one lived beyond reach of redemption. So he went up to the hillside to his mine where he had dug and looked one day to find gold. He swung his axe into its timbers so that the walls fell in and soil flowed down and closed the door. Then he knew that not he nor any man would enter there again.

He came back to his cabin. He took his bed and table and bench outside into the clearing and made a pile of them, with his pack-saddles and bridles, and all his blankets, except only one which he kept for himself. Then he brought brush-wood and made a great fire, which smouldered a long time before his door. He walked out to his four horses, where he heard the bell, caught them, tied them and shot them, and left them there in the forest.

As he returned to the clearing two men rode into it with their pack-horses. They were travelling from the south down the river towards Edmonton, and meant to pass a night with Red Rorty. They had heard the shots back in the timber and now saw the fire before the cabin, and looking in through the open door saw that it was empty.

One of them, who was leading, called out to Red Rorty.

"Hi, Red!" he cried. "What are you doing – are your blankets lousy?"

Red Rorty, approaching, stopped and dropped the butt of his rifle to the ground before he answered.

"What I do," he said, "is my business."

"But, man, to burn your blankets and pack-saddles . . . ?"

"What I do is my business. I answer to no man. This much I will tell you, that I am cleaning my house, and that it would suit you well to do likewise. These things that I burn are for to-day. I live for to-morrow and for the days that come after."

As he spoke the wind parted his beard and blew it back against his shoulders. He rubbed his fingers into his eyes, still tender, and which watered in the sunlight so that he stood before the two riders with tears on his cheeks.

Then his hand fell back to his rifle and he filled his lungs and shouted, and his voice roamed wild in the valley: "Get out of here and leave me! Go home and clean your houses! – for you, and all like you, are God-forsaken and damned!"

They left him then, though their backs felt cold when they were turned. Down the trail in the timber they found his horses dead upon the ground, each his nose against a tree, held there by a halter. They rode on into Edmonton, and when they got there they said Red Rorty had shot his horses, burned his saddles and blankets and the things in his cabin. He talked like a madman, they said, and soon would be shaking hands with the willows. Men spoke of that for a while and shook their heads and laughed. Then other things came which were newer, and they forgot Red Rorty who was shaking hands with the willows.

Of the Indians who had come to the cabin to trade their furs with Red Rorty there were three tribes. There were the Crees, who came from the north. They were a good people, and no men were so wise as they were in river water. There were the Stoneys, who came on horseback from far to the south, and who fought with the Crees. They were strong men, and fond of boasting. Both these people had had priests among them and so were able to curse in the white man's way. They used rifles, too, and the Stoneys had white men's saddles for their horses.

The others who came were the Shuswaps. They came from the west, past Yellowhead Pass – a small tribe, peaceful, and not ready with big words. They had no horses, but walked and hunted with spears and bows and arrows as their fathers had hunted, and the men wore the robes of marmot skins their fathers had worn. Often they hungered. Though their village on the other side of the mountains was close to the fur-trail the early brigades had travelled, no priest had come to them. Red Rorty had learned to speak the language of all these people, even that of the Shuswaps, which was difficult and distinct from the others.

He had now nothing left in his cabin but the floor – worn smooth by his feet – to sleep on, a little meat, and some flour. The meat and the flour he threw upon the fire. Then he shut the door and locked it, and with his rifle on his arm and his blanket laid across his back, turned west to the pass at Yellowhead and to the Shuswap people, for he believed that his life now lay in that direction and that he would teach The Way even as Paul had set out for Macedonia and farther places and taught the people there.

This was in 1880 in the summer.

The Shuswap people lived where the valley of the Fraser opened wide and handsome. It was a great flat where pine-trees grew, and among the pine-trees were meadows of black soil and grass. On three sides it was surrounded by mountains, forested to their tops. On the north side rose Robson's Peak, a great mountain, capped with ice and snow, and the only one in the region named. By French- and English-speaking travellers in the mountains the Shuswaps were sometimes called the *Tête Jaune*, or Yellowhead people, and the place where they lived was known as *Tête Jaune Cache*, from their belief that one day a leader would come among them – a tall man (for they were of short stature) with yellow hair, and lead them back over the mountains to their cousins, the Salish tribes along the coast, from whom in the first place they stemmed. No one knew how the belief had begun among them, but it was a strong belief and gave its name to their district and, in English, to the pass to the east.

In the summers the Shuswaps lived in houses made of brush, their fires set beyond the doorways. Before the snow came they went underground for the warmth, digging great holes and supporting the sides with poles from the forest. They covered the roofs with sod, making a space where the smoke from their fires escaped and where men entered and left, using the trunk of a small tree, some branches left on it for foothold, as a ladder. They had for food deer, moose, and mountain-goat, when they could find them, and marmot, squirrels, and wood-rats when times were bad. They ate, too, bulbs of the mountain lily, wild onions and parsnip, which they baked in an oven under the ground over heated stones covered with grass. They baked cakes from the inner bark of the cedar-tree. They made baskets from birch bark and pine bark to carry berries plucked from the bushes and bring water from the river up to the village.

Red Rorty walked for three days to come to them, and in his travel he hungered, for his hands were no longer steady and he found game hard to hit with his rifle. He took fish from the creeks and ate berries that grew along the trail. Sometimes he knelt before a mountain and prayed God to guide him.

Before he arrived the Shuswap people heard of his coming and made ready to receive him. They built a fresh brushwood shelter where he would sleep, and a fire of his own to warm him, and a meal of young goat-meat and herbs for him to eat. Tzalas, one of them who had been to the Athabaska and who knew him, went out to meet him and bring him to the village.

He stayed with them, and the people were glad, for they believed that he was a great man; and some of them said that he was the leader with yellow hair who had come to take them back over the mountains to a land full of game, fish in all the rivers, and berries growing by each man's door. They remembered the Shuswaps had once been a strong people, living in houses wide and long as rivers, with great feasts and dances.

The women laid him fresh boughs to sleep on each night, brought wood for his fire and food for him to eat. He stayed with them, and sometimes forgot why in the first place he had come. It seemed, when he remembered, that the Athabaska valley was in flames when he left it, and that men moved behind those flames with rifles. They called his name, and when they found him they would shoot him, and leave his bones for the coyotes to pick.

At times at night in the stillness with the people lying about their fires, each man wrapped in his robe, alone like the separate spokes of a wagon wheel, Red Rorty thought he heard his name called, softly, close to where he slept. He would awake with a yell, rousing the village. He then made his fire higher and sat by it till morning. The people believed that these were visions that woke him from his sleep, and waited for him to speak.

Then one day his faith grew strong and compelled him.

He gathered the people about him below a black cliff at the edge of the flats. They sat on the ground, the men near to him and behind them the women and children. There were thirty families in all, so that he spoke to a great concourse of people. He told them of Jesus Christ, of His works, and that He would come again one day to be a leader of mankind.

"Only those who believe," Red Rorty said, "will be saved. All the rest will be destroyed, and before they are destroyed they will see their children born armless, and on the foreheads of those children, that should be clean and shining, coarse, thick hair will grow."

When he had spoken the people said that no man had spoken with such a great voice before. He threw his voice up against the rock cliffs beyond them, and it stayed there and murmured till they heard him speaking to them from above and behind, while they beheld him standing, his mouth moving and his shadow upon the ground before them.

All the people wondered. Some were angry to think that this man who spoke was not the leader they hoped for but one who came to speak only of another to come later.

"Still," said Tis-Kwinit, an older man who passed many days alone on the hill-tops fasting, "it may be that he has come to hasten our faith. This leader he speaks of, and our leader we wait for, it seems they are one man and the same – for each comes to lead the people across the mountains to a land that is better than the one we know."

Kwakala, a man great in his magic, who cured with his songs and his beaver-tooth rattle, said: "No, they are two men. One is a stranger and avenger. But our leader will have yellow hair, and we will know him. He comes to lead us, not to destroy us."

Tzalas spoke. He was the best hunter, a strong man, and other men listened to his words.

"It is better," he said, "that we cleave to our own leader who knows us and who will call us all by the names we are given. If we go elsewhere to search for another, when he comes he will find the valley deserted. He will be alone, and wander the mountains."

Still the people talked by their fires and in their houses, and no man could tell whither they were turning.

In those days the men were busy with their hunting, and some days many were gone from the village. The women, too, went back into the hills with their baskets to return laden with the fibre of cedar-trees. This they beat with sticks, then, parting their skirts, rubbed it between the palms of their hands and their thighs till it shredded into yarn and dropped into the baskets at their feet. From this and goat-wool they made the long garments they wore.

One of these women was called Hanni. She was a young woman, wife of Swamas, who was gone on a long trip back into the mountains to hunt the caribou. She had hair that was plaited and fell to her waist, and her breasts, full and heavy, moved beneath her dress when she walked. She was thought gentle and a good woman, yet she was sad because she had promised Swamas that she would bear him a male child, and though they had been married two summers she was still not a mother.

Red Rorty saw her standing one day beneath a pine-tree shredding cedar bark into the basket by her feet. Her thigh was bare, and, oiled with the cedar, shone in the sunlight. Her roving hand caressed it. He looked upon it with longing, for his flesh was lonely.

Later, when it was dusk and people had laid themselves by their fires to sleep, Hanni passed close to his house on the edge of the clearing. He came out and seized her, brought her into his house. She did not resist. His troubled flesh found ease.

The next day when the people learned what had happened they were angry, for among them a woman had one man and a man one woman and no other. They broke down Red Rorty's house. They trampled it under their feet and fired its brush. The women beat him with sticks and stones, and drove him from them into the forest, for they said if he had needed a woman there were other women he might have gone to who were without husbands.

They followed Red Rorty into the forest then, the women and some children with them. They caught him, and, with long damp ropes of cedar bark, bound him with his back to the trunk of a pine-tree. They bound his hands behind the trunk, and his feet also, bending his legs about the tree, and put a stout thong about his neck to hold it tight and unmoving so that in a way he was kneeling, although no part of him touched the ground.

They ripped his clothes from his body and touched the white flesh, a thing of wonder, and laughed when their nails brought the red blood out upon it. The children stood back and shot small arrows into his belly.

Then one of the women ran to the village and returned with fire, and Yaada, the sister of Hanni, seized the brand and held it for a while below Red Rorty's beard, till the beard and his long brown hair took fire, and the flame, like a breath he exhaled, rose above his head and licked the bark of the tree. With the fire his mouth opened to shout but no sound came from it. Yaada took a round small stone and shoved it between his jaws, and it stayed there, as a word he tried to utter, while the flames began to roar around him.

The tree to which he was tied took fire and others about it, until there was a wide swath there in the forest where the flames raged. They burned for three days, and left the ground black and tree-trunks withered and smoking. While the ground was yet hot and smouldered, Yaada and some others returned.

They found the skull, fallen to the ground and caught in the black twisted roots of a tree. The stone was still between its jaws. Yaada took a stick and pointed.

"See!" she said, "he was a great liar, and the word has choked him!"

TWO

S till, when Red Rorty had gone from them the people were not happy.

They had waited long seasons for their leader with yellow hair to come among them, and he had not come. The big bearded man from the Athabaska spoke to them of another, who was also a leader, and promised that he would come soon, in a man's life, to lead them to a new country and make them brothers with all mankind. These were words they wished to hear.

For in those days, too, the people waited to be told what to believe. Their faith was the substance of things hoped for, the shadow of what they could not yet discern. They believed that the world was made of things they could not touch nor see, as they knew that behind the basket their hands made was the shape of the perfect basket which once made would endure for ever and beyond the time when its semblance was broken and worn thin by use. So they knew that the shape of to-morrow lingered just beyond to-day, and that to-day the people made to-morrow's basket. Each man hoped to see what his hands were doing, and no man could. Each man sought the shadow beyond his work, and no man could reach it. But this man from the Athabaska told them that he could see to-morrow and that a leader was coming to them. And that was their belief, because it was what they hoped for.

The Shuswap people, their fathers said, had been led far into the mountains by one who was a bad leader, who promised game where there was little, and fish where the big fish rotted on their way up the rivers. The bellies of their hunters had become slack, their children's legs were weak, and their old men died too soon. The stranger's words had brought them faith that fatter days would come, and they feared that when he went away he had taken his words with him and that they would believe no longer.

And the winter that came when he had gone was hard. Swamas, the husband of Hanni, came back. He and his men had gone far. They had hunted beyond the Always-Smoking River. They found nothing, until returning they killed two cow caribou, as thin as themselves, and a black wolf with the hair gone from his tail. They said the spirits of the caribou and the moose and the deer had been offended. Each man then asked himself what he had done – had he always spoken gently to an animal before killing it – had he taken all its meat, leaving none upon the ground – had he buried the bones before he came away so that they might come forth again clothed in flesh and hide? And all men had done what they should do, except that some said Mingqaias, a young man new to his hunting and one who had not gone out with Swamas, when he killed his she-bear he had failed to hang the head in a tree after its killing, for this was the way with a bear, which has a powerful spirit and magic. Then the hunters said the bear-spirit had been offended. Mingqaias, they said, could hunt no more, and would therefore wear the clothes of a woman.

There were others who said the game fled from the hunters because the stranger from the Athabaska had been chased from the village and killed. It was his spirit that, returning, had turned the game from the hunters. Some spoke against Hanni for this, and she was sent for a time to live alone in a brush shelter beyond the village.

In that winter when the people, as was their custom when the snow came, went to live in their houses under the ground there was little food. Sometimes a hunter would bring in a rabbit, or some grouse, or a few thin fish caught through the ice of the lakes. Then for a time the people's mouths would be wet and they would be happy. But at other times men and women would rise up from their houses through the snow in the morning like bodies from the grave and go from one smoke-hole to another and call down for food for their children or their old people – because in such times each family shared and helped the others as in better times what they owned was held in common. There were women weeping, and children with no strength who yet played their games chirping and hopping like birds, and hunters standing silent to look up on the mountains where they could see no life. At night the people sat below around their fires and listened to the wind in the trees. There each man could hear the voice-spirits of dead hunters calling to one another as they pursued spirit deer and moose overhead in the darkness. Many cradle baskets were hung up in the trees around the village that winter, where the women, sorrowing, had put them to be used no more, and men could hear these, too, hitting against the branches when the voices of the dead hunters rode by on the wind.

Then Mingqaias, who had offended the bear-spirit, had a vision. He dreamed, he said, that he saw two beautiful maidens with long hair sitting on a grassy ridge in the sunlight. They called to him and he went up and sat between them. They talked to him, and he saw that they were no longer maidens, but two doe deer. The bodies of those deer, he said, were fat, and their coats shone in the sun. The deer told him that a great hunter and great leader was coming among his people and that he would come soon. He would be called Kumkan-Kleseem, for he would be tall and his hair yellow as the poplar leaves in the early frost.

Mingqaias related his vision, and the old men shook their heads. Mingqaias, they said, was a liar. Everyone in the village knew he was a liar.

"The face of Kumkan-Kleseem," some began to say, "is like the face of the west wind. It warms the blood of the people. But no man will ever see it."

Later, after the snow when the ground was green, the people came back up out of their houses and lived once more in their bough shelters beneath the trees. Game returned to the hunters, and berries were in the women's baskets.

Then when the days were already long Hanni, the wife of Swamas, who was with child, took to her bed and would not rise. The three old women, come to attend to her when the child was born, said that unless she rose she would surely die.

Hanni called for Swamas.

She said, "Swamas, I will die and my child with me, for the sickness that has entered me is a big sickness and its life is stronger than mine."

Swamas said, "You will not die. You are not yet ready to die. You have not lived a woman's life until you have borne your child, and until you have lived your life you cannot die."

"Nevertheless, Swamas, I will die."

"If you die," answered Swamas, "that part of me, which

is yours, will die with you. But you will not die. Nor will I die, for new life is coming to us."

Then Swamas called Kwakala, who came and played for three nights on his reed and rattled his rattles of beaver-teeth for three days that the sickness might leave her. He pushed burning splinters into her stomach where the pain was. He made a likeness of the sickness and burned it behind her shelter. Still the sickness was not frightened and did not leave her.

On the fourth day when the three old women who had come to prepare her for the birth of the child sat by the fire beyond her door and moaned, and while her father, the old man, Smutuksen, stood under a tree and waited, and Kwakala sat within and shook his rattle, Hanni sent again for Swamas, who was near by alone fasting for these days to help her.

"Swamas," she said, "the sickness grows bigger. Beside it my spirit is uneasy. Soon my spirit will leave me."

Swamas sat and said nothing. Kwakala held his rattle and waited.

After a while, Hanni said, "It is cold."

Swamas said, "The sun is high. The day is warm."

Later while the sun still was high, Hanni said, "It is night. Darkness is about me. Come close. I am afraid. Speak to me loudly for my head lies on a river."

Swamas, beside her, answered nothing.

Soon Kwakala said, "I see her spirit rising from her body."

He went outside and watched her spirit rise above the tree-tops. Then Swamas left the place and painted his face black. He cut his hair short, and put twigs of the fir-tree in his belt. For many moons of mourning he could not fish nor hunt, nor put his shadow before another, and would sleep with his head on nettles, his bed fenced by a picket of spruce.

The old women took the baskets Hanni had used to gather berries and cedar bark from the hillsides, and the white bone-needles for her sewing, and everything that was hers, and hid them in the forest, for they should be touched no more. The basket she had made for the child they hung high on a tree along the trail to the river that the child's spirit might see it and be happy.

When the people had mourned over her for three days, on the fourth day they took her body, wrapped in burial clothes of cedar bark and goat's-wool, and buried it in the soft earth at the foot of a slide. They left food by the grave that she might not be hungry. The night after the burial there was a feast. It was a good feast, and afterwards many of the people retched and were sick on the ground.

But the spirit of Swamas was sad. For many days still he was without food and without drink. Each night he went to the grave, made his bed there and slept upon it until the sun came to wake him. The people were grieved at seeing him without solace in his sorrow. His mother spoke to him, and brought him good food to eat. Then he ate, but his hands were idle, and he would find no work to do. His eyes became the eyes of an old man who looks far and sees nothing. His face deepened till it was like a cave, and people feared to see into it. His body thinned. Hair fell from his head, and his bones shook from the night cold of the grave.

Yet each night he went there and slept away from his people, till the snow came and covered the grave and he could go no more.

The warm winds returned, leaves sprouted again on the poplar-trees, and Swamas went once more to the grave where his wife lay buried. On the grave he saw a small boy gathering firewood. He entered the grave and came out again to gather the blue and yellow flowers from beneath the trees, then returned to his place under the ground. Swamas watched a long time, his eyes kindling, yet he did not speak. He went home that night to the food his mother brought him, and was silent.

Then the next day he went up into the forest on the mountain side to find birch wood, from which he fashioned four small bows. These he brought back to the village where the people were happy to see him at work once again.

Swamas went out towards the grave and planted the bows apart from each other on the path leading towards the village. The boy came out from the grave and saw the small bows up-ended. He reached for the first one and took it with him back under the ground. For the next bow he had to go farther from the grave into the pine-trees and closer to the village. Yet he took it too, and the others as well. Swamas watched the boy moving over the new green grass, through the blue and yellow flowers and the willows with their leaves just broken from the bud. He saw that the boy's hair was yellow. He smiled, and his heart that had hung like a dead bird within his breast fluttered then beat fast once more.

The next day he planted four more bows, and on the third day four more after that. At first the boy was small and could carry only one bow with him at a time to the grave. Soon he took two, and the last day he took the four together under his arm and carried them away with him.

Then Swamas told the twelve wise old men of the village what he had seen and what he had done. That night they sat and talked around their fire while Kwakala shook his rattle and sang. Swamas did as they bade him.

After three days he planted twelve bows leading from the grave to the village, each bow as it approached the village larger than the one before it. The last one he planted outside the spruce shelter where the twelve wise men sat, and it was as tall as the doorway by which it stood. Inside the shelter Swamas was with the wise men, who burned sweet-smelling grass on their fire to give them magic, and each one while they waited made his own medicine. Kwakala was there with them too.

They watched through the openings in the sides of the shelter, and when the boy came for the last bow of all, which was heavy so that his body bent beneath it, Kwakala, who was the farthest on in his magic, ran out and pursued him and caught him by the edge of the grave where he was about to descend for the last time. He brought him back to the other wise men.

But when he reached the shelter where the others waited the boy's body shrivelled to almost nothing so that Kwakala's hands held only a few wisps of yellow hair. Then for three days the wise men sang and shook rattles and blew on the wisps of yellow hair that at times were so few and thin that they thought they had been deceived and saw nothing and had nothing between them. But on the fourth day the boy became truly alive.

Still he was not happy, and cried. His cries travelled through the village, and for many days the people were disturbed. The men could not hunt, nor the women prepare food for them to eat. The wise men seemed wise no more, and were at a loss to comfort the child. They gave him fresh red berries to eat, and beaver tail, and the nose of a young cow moose, and the fat from the kidney of a kid brought down from the mountain-top. Still he cried, and was not happy.

Then Tzalas remembered and went many days' journey over the mountains to where a wise woman lived with another tribe. He brought her back with him, and the wise men promised to pay her with goat's-wool, of which her tribe had none, if she would cure the child of his weeping. So she took the boy and held him. She went out with him, and walked through the forest and listened to him. When she came back to the twelve wise men she laughed.

"I thought," she said, "it was something big and great the child was wanting. What he wants is only a little thing. He wants the full, free life of a man – not the half-life he had in the grave."

She said further: "He wants his cousin – that is, Memhaias, son of Yaada, sister of Hanni – to go with him up yonder mountain where the great spruce-trees grow, and the people to set fire to the spruce-trees so that the gum may fall on the bodies of them both as they stand underneath. Then the people must wash him and his cousin beneath a waterfall."

It was done as the boy wanted, and as the old woman said. That night Swamas held a great feast, with much meat, for the game had come close to see what was happening in the village that the hunters had so long forgotten them. The people were happy, and danced and sang, and Kwakala played on his reed, and the young men beat drums around the fire, for all felt that surely something great had come into their midst and that the days that were before them would bring a change in their lives. They ate much, and many were sick close to Swamas that he might know his feast was bigger than the bellies of the people.

From the beginning they called the boy Kumkan-Kleseem, and later Kumkleseem, for his yellow head. The young women and the old women quarrelled with one another to comb his hair and to bathe him. Still for a long time the wise woman from the tribe across the mountains stayed, for he clung to her and was content when she was near. Over the grave at the foot of the slide they piled rocks lest one day, seeing the way back whence he had come he should leave them – for, though he cried no more, he was not yet happy as other children, and there were those who thought he still felt strange above the ground with the voices of men and women about him and that his spirit hungered for the darkness of the grave.

Then his cousin, Memhaias, who was with him much, noticed one day why the boy was not as other children, and did not laugh with them as they played through the village. He called his mother, Yaada, to see, and she called the old wise woman who was with them from across the mountains, and soon the twelve wise men came and gathered round and saw. At first some were fearful, and would have moved the village and left the boy – for they saw that on the ground he had no shadow. He walked in the sunlight as other children, but alone with no shadow to follow him and protect him. For this he was sad, and his lips had not learned the way of laughter.

Kwakala came and shook his head. Strong in magic, he knew his magic was not strong enough. The wise men talked but were in sorrow, for they said that without his shadow the boy was still not truly among them.

"He has left his shadow in the grave," they said. Still there was none among them, nor in the village, brave enough to pull back the stones and go down for it. The people feared, too, that if the grave were opened the boy might go down into it and not come up again.

Then the wise old woman spoke, laughing:

"It is nothing," she said. "In the grave the boy had no shadow. He was not born as other children between the ground and the sun where his shadow could find him. His shadow still waits for him, and he must find it."

So she took the child with her on to the top of the high mountain in the east, where the shadows come from in the morning and where they return at night. She was there with him three nights in the home of the shadows till she found one shadow which was alone.

On the fourth day, when the sun rode high, she brought the boy back to the village. He stood apart and solitary with his shadow.

At first it was a small shadow, and short and faint upon the ground. But the people saw it, and were amazed. They came close that they might better see it. And when they came close there was no shadow, for one man stepped upon it and it left him.

Then the old woman took Kumkleseem back again into the east to the home of the shadows, and she waited there for three days with him, and came back on the fourth day with the boy and his shadow. And this time the people who saw were afraid, and stood back from him, that no one might touch his shadow.

And the shadow that at first was a small shadow, faint upon the ground, held to him and grew with the days till it was black and heavy, and men said the grasses moved when it passed upon them. In the days to come when Kumkleseem was still a boy, and later when he grew to be a man, the people were careful not to tread upon his shadow nor to touch it, fearful that it would leave him and that without the old woman to help them they would be unable to find it again and bring it to him.

The old woman left, and returned home with many baskets of goat-wool to her tribe across the mountains, and Kumkleseem lived with his cousin Memhaias in the house of Yaada, who was the sister of Hanni. He learned to shoot with the bow and arrow, and to catch rabbits with a snare, and to kill grouse with a willow stick. He played with the other children, and laughed with them at their games. Yet they could not do with him quite as with the others, for always when he came close to them they would hold their eyes to the ground to make way for his shadow. So men said that, while it was true the boy Kumkleseem laughed and played with his fellows in the day, it was when the sun was gone and his shadow had left him for the night that he seemed most happy, for it was then that he could come close to his people.

The boy remained. He grew strong, swift of foot and a good hunter. He grew tall, till his head, wondrous fair with hair, and shining, rose above those around him.

THREE

When Kumkleseem approached manhood the people waited, for this was the time when the boy would cease to exist and the man come into being. The boy was a child with a child's spirit that moved and lived in a land of his own creating. He could be taught, but he must not be commanded, for the eyes of those around him, who were older, no longer saw the visions of his eyes, and the places that he went to were no longer the places they could enter.

But the boy must die and the man be born to live in the world that other men have made. The boy says "I." The man says "We" – and this word that the man speaks is the word of his greatest magic.

Kumkleseem had done all things that a boy should do. In his hunting, when camp was moved, he waited till the others had gone far that, running to overtake them, his legs would become hard and his breath learn to stay with him and not be left behind in the running. Each day he went to the cold river-water, in the winter into the snow, and when he came out was beaten with sticks of willow. At night, after the frosts, he lay outside naked away from the fires with no robe around him till the morning, and many a night he lay on the river-bank with his hands in the water. He had become the swiftest runner and the surest hunter of his fellows. He had learned with them the teachings of his people – that it was bad to speak untruthfully, to steal, to be lazy, to lie with a woman till she had become his own, or to boast if he was not a great man.

Still he was not fully a man, nor in their society which would bind him, protect him, compel him, till he had gone away from the people to a place of his choosing, to sit alone without food for a period of days that he might have a vision to show him the shape and the colour of the life before him, and to know the spirit that would guide him. So the people waited that Kumkleseem might choose, for in his choosing they hoped for a sign, and in his vision they hoped to see somewhat of the path beyond them.

Now in those days close to the village, to the south below the sun when it was high, was a valley into which no man went. The water that came down from that valley was turgid, dark, and flowed silently, with no rapids. It was said that if a man drank of that water he would lose his voice and go from the sight of his fellows, roaming the hills at night to bark at the moon like a coyote. The coyote men saw by day was not the same they heard by night, for the coyote they heard by night was the voice of a man whose hands had become claws and whose teeth had grown long and tusk-like, who sat on his haunches, lifted his head to the sky and lamented the human speech gone from him.

The spirit of that valley was cruel. Men feared that one night, taking the form of a great white bear, it would come down upon them in their sleep and leave them with a coyote's howl for voice and only a coyote's claws for hands, and each man would be for ever a stranger to his neighbour. It was a real fear and not a fear to be lightened by laughter. So for three nights when the moon was dark they beat drums around their fires to frighten the spirit of the valley, and on the fourth night they had a feast and danced slowly round in a circle.

When the time had come for Kumkleseem, and the people saw him sitting on a ridge and gazing up that valley, their eyes followed and were sad, for they knew where his thoughts were leading. Yet they could not do anything, for he stood now in the river-fork.

Still, on the night before he left them, Smutuksen, grown old and weak, with a stick to support him, took Kumkleseem beyond the village into a clearing in the forest. He lifted his stick and pointed above to the sky.

"There," he said, "above you – the big one. Do you see him?"

"I see him."

"That is The Bear. You see him, and he sees you."

Then Smutuksen was happy, for he thought he had put strength in the heart of the boy. They returned to the village.

On the next day Kumkleseem went out and walked alone into the valley. He was gone for twelve days. No one would follow after him to care for him, for each of them feared. On the twelfth night of his fasting he returned.

The men of the village were seated round the fire. He seated himself among them. They waited for him to speak of his vision and of what he had seen in the valley. Food was placed beside him which he would not touch until he had spoken.

"You have come far," said Tis-Kwinit, who, when he was young, sat naked four days on a mountain-top.

"I have gone far," answered Kumkleseem.

"You have seen great things."

"My eyes that have seen little are tired with what they saw."

Then Tis-Kwinit dropped his eyes and was silent. Tzalas, who was next, spoke to Kumkleseem, whose face grown lean and hard with his journey, gleamed against the fire, and whose eyes sparkled with hunger, and whose yellow hair, long to his shoulders, lifted gently and flowed out from him in the night wind of the forest.

"The words you have heard," said Tzalas, "the visions you have seen, you will tell us."

Kumkleseem said, "I left you. I went alone up the dark valley. I went for four days till I could go no farther. Then I waited and listened for four days more. On the ninth day I turned back the way I had come. Now I am here."

"What you say is good," said Tzalas.

"It is good," said Smutuksen, who leaned forward, the point of his stick pressed into the hot rim of the fire. "It is good, but we would know more. Your eyes went with you and your ears. What have they remembered of your journey?"

For some time Kumkleseem was silent. Then he spoke again.

"As you say, my eyes were with me and my ears. On the end of the fourth day my eyes told me I could go no farther. I had come to where the river is born, and where a man could step across it. Rock walls were before me. Ice hung upon them – white, and cold as an old woman's breast. One place there was where a man might still go on, but I knew I had come to the end of my journey. I did the thing that I should do. Against a spruce-tree, withered by lightning long ago, on some sand the river had fallen away from, I sat and waited and my eyes watched and my ears listened. Close to me I saw in the green coarse grass the place where a cow moose had borne her calf three days before. Closer to me still, so that I could see the broken tips of the willows in the sun, an old moose had browsed. Earlier, when the snow had just left the ground, a she-bear and her two cubs had crossed on the sand past my feet, for the marks were there before me. On the ledges above my head goats came when the day was warm and lay down in the sun. The rest I saw was grass trembling in the wind, and the roof of the forest bending when the mountains breathed, and sun shining on running water.

"At night in the darkness I felt the mountains come closer so that they were against my elbows, and my bones that could not move were sore and aching. At night the river spoke loudly. An owl, the soul of a departed woman, was in the tree above me, and my ears, become lonely, were tender to its message. Mice ran over my toes. On the first morning after I was there below the spruce-tree I saw that a marten had been beside me in the night. On the second morning a lynx. On the third morning a great black wolf, and on the fourth morning, of the day that I turned back to the village, I saw that an old bear, with snow-dust on his coat, had made his bed beyond my feet, and stayed there the night, his head upon his forepaws to watch me, for in the morning he left his shape and shreds of fur behind him."

When Kumkleseem had spoken this, Squeleken, the oldest of the old men and the most wise, stood and said: "It is well. You have spoken with the words of a man. The bear-spirit will be your guardian spirit. His strength will be your strength, and his cunning yours. His mark will be upon you, and your mark upon him. He will pull back the cape from his face so that you may see him, and he will talk to you with a man's voice."

Swamas, who was there too, smiled and was happy.

Squeleken went back to his place, and Smutuksen, remembering the night before Kumkleseem went from them up the valley, rose and said: "Squeleken speaks well the words I have already spoken. Yet we who are here would know more. The Yellowhead has told us much, still he has told us little. His eyes have seen much, but his ears have heard little. He has seen only what another man might see, and has heard less than another man might hear. Is there no word he has left in the valley and feared to bring down to us who have waited?"

After a while Kumkleseem said: "There was a word. There was a voice. I heard speech in the trees. It called me farther than I had gone. Still I turned my face from it for I had gone as far as my return would let me. One voice, alone, yet lost in the rest, bade me stay lest I go so far I would not come back. I feared, and I stayed."

At this men wondered, and among them were those who sorrowed. Some of them asked if the valley had cast its spell upon Kumkleseem so that he no longer spoke to them wholly with a man's tongue, for these were words they did not understand. Others, remembering his birth, were afraid that he might still go from them and leave them, fearing that the darkness of the earth, where he lived before they knew him, had stained his spirit.

Kumkleseem spoke again. "That you may know where I have been," he said, "and see that I am not a liar, I have brought back with me sand from the bank of the river where I fasted."

He held up before them for all to see a bag sewn from the soft belly-skin of a caribou. It was heavy. He tilted it. Sand flowed out and spread itself upon the ground between his knees.

He said, "It is the dark sand where the dark waters come

from." He ran his fingers through it, and let it fall before the firelight.

"It is heavy," he said, "heavier than any sand that I have known. It is dark, yet the light of the sun has entered into it so that it shines even now at night."

The men came closer and saw that what he said was true. They cupped the sand in their hands. They smelled it. They laid their tongues upon it. They spat it out.

"It is bitter," said Tzalas, "like the meat from the neck of a mountain-goat long dead. Yet there may be magic in it, for it is the sand where the dark river comes from."

Then Kumkleseem gathered it up and put it back into the bag. It was his, and not to be shared with others.

And that night and the next day and the next night after that, till the sun brought the shadows down again from the mountain, there was a great feast and the noise of drums among the hunters and the old men of the village, for Kumkleseem, no longer a boy, walked as a man before them.

That day, while the men still rested from their feasting, strangers approached the village. A boy came running to Tzalas who sat alone, half sleeping, by the fire side.

"White men are coming," he said. "Three white men and six horses. They are tired, and have travelled far. I have seen them."

When the white men came the people gathered about to see them and their horses, for the people were poor and had no horses and wondered at men who could walk with their feet above the grass tops. The white men wore the dust of long travel. They were hungry and ate, after loosing their horses where the grass grew high to their bellies.

One of them who was older, black-bearded and darker in the eyes and skin, spoke the tongue of the people, and turned his words to Tzalas who stood waiting. He took from his pocket a piece of hide, laid it upon the ground and showed Tzalas that on it were the likeness of mountains and of the rivers that flow through them and of the forests that grow in the valleys. Tzalas marvelled that white men should know so much. He listened to the words spoken.

"We have come a long distance," the white man said, "and we are still far from the end of our journey. We are peace-lovers, and no harm rides with us. Here on this hide you see where we stand, and here" – his finger pointed – "you see where we would go."

The white man stood then and pointed south to the dark valley whence Kumkleseem had returned from his fasting. His two fellows came forward – tall men, with red faces, big hands and big feet, like twins who command the weather – to talk with him while he listened.

The white man who knew the words of the people, turned once more to Tzalas and pointed.

"Yes, up there, to that valley is where we would go with our horses. We want that one man from among you, who has been there and knows how the water runs, should go with us."

Tzalas shook his head. That valley, he said, was a valley where no man would go. Its water was bad water and the people feared to drink it. Only one man from among them had been there, and that for his fasting.

Then the white man said, "And this man, who is he? Ask him to come to me that we may talk."

Kumkleseem came forward. The white man spoke to him and asked him to go with them up the valley.

"There is nothing up the valley," said Kumkleseem. "I have been there and I have seen. I have gone there till I could go no farther. I fasted, and came back. There is nothing there but the place where my body sat. The water that flows there is black. That you may know I am not a liar, that my words are the words of a man and not spoken to you by a boy, I will show you sand from the bank where I rested. It is the sand from which the dark river runs."

He took his bag, opened it, and emptied the sand that glistened on the ground between the white man's feet.

The two white men, who had been silent, stepped forward and knelt. Each ran his hand through it, weighed it, lifted it so that it fell through his curved fingers and melted once more on the ground. They talked in their language. They laughed. They hit each other upon the shoulders until the people thought they were fighting. Tzalas stood close and wondered at the magic of the sand.

The white man spoke again. If Kumkleseem would go with them they would give him a rifle that would kill a moose with its voice as far away as he could see. They would give him bullets and powder, and a coat to wear, red as bear's blood.

Kumkleseem went with them, and was gone for three full moons. He returned with the white men, who went away, back along the path that they first had come. They left with Kumkleseem the rifle, the bullets, the red coat, and with the people bright cloth and beads, knives, and flint and steel. The white men were happy. They sang on their horses, which were weak with the journey, their backs raw with the saddles.

When Kumkleseem returned he was no longer Kumkleseem. In the village the white man who spoke the tongue of the people, and the others who spoke little, called him not Kumkleseem, which was the name his own people had given him, but spoke to him by the new name of *Tête Jaune*.

"Tête Jaune," the white man told Tzalas, "is a good man. He is strong. His eyes are good. The mountains are his friends."

The people thought the white men had given Kumkleseem the new name for deeds he had done on his journey. They were proud that he should have a second name. Then Kumkleseem said that he wished men to use the new name, which was the name the white men had given to him, and to forget he had been called Kumkleseem.

After a time it was as he wished, and men came to know him as Tête Jaune. But the name – strange to their tongues – was spoken as *Tay John*. Those of the old men who had been with him when he was young remembered him only as Kumkleseem, and found this new name too sharp for speech.

White men came again; more than once, to the village. Always they asked for Tay John of whom they had heard from their fellows. He went with them to show them the way through the mountains, or to take some of them up the dark river. Sometimes they returned with him, to follow their tracks back to the east. Sometimes, after many days' journey, he returned to the village alone and the white men passed on over the mountains and were seen no more by the people. Soon Tay John knew the words of the white man and stood between them and the people. The people, seeing him with all men's words on his tongue, were glad, for they thought that, grown great in the village through his travel, among others he was a great man, too.

Tay John now walked alone among them. His yellow hair marked his different birth. His rifle was his own, and no man could touch it. His red coat was a sign of the white man's favour. His name was no more the name come from his people but the name he had earned when he was far from them.

Days came when the young men, following Tay John, failed to hunt meat and hides for the village. They began now to hunt other animals than the moose, caribou, goat and deer –

smaller animals deep in the timber; the marten, the lynx, the mink and the fox, and to pack the fur on their backs to traders across the mountains. The women's hands hung idle from their shoulders with no skins to sew and no wool to make into clothes. The young men came back from their trading with red scarves and sashes, and some of them with rifles.

Yet, though they had rifles, the game, when hunger forced them to go for it, was harder to come upon than when they had hunted it with bow and arrow. As the white men came closer the game drew back into the mountains. Children and the old people hungered in the village, and the hunters grew lean on the hills. People wondered, and some of them questioned, wearied in their waiting for a sign from Kumkleseem, the man they now knew as Tay John.

Some men said they should move the village to follow the game back into the mountains. But Smutuksen, Tzalas, and others, whose faith was still the servant of their hopes, said they would wait a while longer and Tay John would lead them. When he was ready he would speak with a great voice and they would go whither his finger pointed.

So the people waited, blind in time, not knowing what the days would bring, but hoping. And while they waited Tay John moved in and out among them, always leaving, still always returning, making great loops through the mountains, till the pattern of his travels reached out from the village like the petals of a flower.

FOUR

One summer, when the berries were almost ripe, a great sickness came among the people. They called it the black sickness, because the bodies of those who died were black. Children and the old people and many of the women were sick. They coughed. They sneezed – and at this they feared, for when a man sneezed his spirit was going from him. Their skin burned, and sores came out upon it. The village stank with those who were sick and with bodies not yet buried. The people thought the ground about them was bad, for those who walked upon it died.

Some said that the white man's god had come into the valley, that the game had fled, and that now they must leave the valley too.

Then Kwakala, whose voice carried far in their counsels, sent for the old men and the hunters, among whom were Tay John and Memhaias, to come to him. They came. He bade them sit beside him at some distance from his house, facing into the sunset, with the shadows of trees at their feet.

For a long time Kwakala, who had been fasting, played upon his flute and they waited.

After a while he said, "I have had a vision. A voice spoke to me. It said: 'New shadows are coming into the land. Your fathers lived where you live for many, many winters. They were friends with the place where they lived. They were gentle. They spoke to a deer before they killed it that its spirit might not be offended. They did not boast. Their hunters said when they went to hunt, "We *may* kill a deer." Their women sang songs to the berry spirit, and danced before they went to the bushes for berries at the first of the season.

"'Now it is different. The young men shake their rifles and boast. Still your bellies are empty. The women have become lazy and do not sing. Their berry baskets are empty. Their needles are blunted because the hunters no longer bring them skins to sew. Fires burn low, for wood is hard to find. Now too a great sickness has come among the people. You feed the ground.'"

Kwakala's voice was still, and he thought.

"Then," he said, "I heard no more. But I saw the people. They journeyed. They smiled. They laughed. They were happy. One man from among them spoke to me. He said: 'We go back to our cousins across the mountains. They will remember our names and we will live among them as our fathers lived.' Before the people and leading them was Tay John. After him came Memhaias, his cousin, and the hunters."

Kwakala ceased to speak.

The people believed in Kwakala's vision.

So, on the day after he had spoken the hunters went out to find what game they could. For three days after that there was dancing and feasting, at dawn, at noon, and at sunset. On the fourth day Tay John and Memhaias set out to find the trail the people should follow and where they should camp at night. They went south, yet more to the west than the dark river. They were gone twelve days, and returned on the appointed day.

The women gathered up their fire-tongs, their root and berry baskets, their serving plaques, their robes, their mats. All that they had and lived among they gathered up and took with them, excepting only the brush houses, which were left standing, desolate.

Tay John and Memhaias went first. After them came the hunters, and following the hunters were the women, some few with children in baskets upon their hips and all with burdens upon their shoulders. Kwakala, whose legs with his age had become wood so that he could not walk, sat on the hide of an old moose, stiff and hard, and two women dragged him. As they dragged him he played upon his reed and shook his rattle that the journey they made might be a good one. Children followed behind him, and after them three old women. Last of all came Smutuksen, leaning on his stick, waiting on the hills to ease his frightened heart.

The first days the people were glad. Children laughed and played. Their mothers laughed with them. The old men were happy to make yet another journey before they died. The hunters found deer and rabbits among the pine-trees, the women blueberries.

Soon, though, the trail led into the forest, under high mountains, where the sun shone only at noon. Instead of grass, their feet sank into moss, and instead of bushes of berries their arms brushed against stalks, tall as a man, sharp with thorns. The forest was silent like sleep, and on the moss were no imprints of deer or of moose. Then the people doubted. They spoke to Tay John who was leading.

They said, "Have you taken us away to die in the wilderness? Were there not graves enough where we were? Had the ground become shallow like streams in autumn that we must come here to find moss to cover our bones? It is better to die in a place where we know the trees and the mountains than to loose our spirits in a land of shadow and forest, the sun a stranger by day and the stars fearing to come by night."

Tay John said nothing. He went forward.

As they travelled the strength of Kwakala fell from him, like drops of water falling in the night. His rattle bounced by his side on the moose hide. His reed lay lost, far away in the moss by the trail. The two women who pulled him said his body grew heavy. They feared his spirit looked back.

One night by the fire his eyes sparkled and he spoke. He lifted his arm, but it dropped once more to his side. Tay John came and held it. Kwakala pointed into the dark trees where on the morrow they would go.

"I see green grass," he said, "and sun shining on it. I see a lake, and poplar-trees, and a moose feeding by the lake."

That night while they slept his spirit left him. They buried him on a ridge that rose in the forest. With him they put his rattle, the plaques from which he ate, some roots and bark of the cedar-tree baked in an oven under the ground. They mourned, for he was a man of magic, and his eyes saw when other men were blind.

Tay John led on through the forest. The people became weak, and their file grew long on the trail, until it would happen that those who were first – the young men and the hunters – would make camp and have their sleep and be on their way again in the morning before some of those who were last – the old men and women, Smutuksen among them – had come to where they stopped the night. Three times they stayed to mourn. Three more graves they left behind them. The last one to die was Yaada, mother of Memhaias.

Then Tay John stopped where the forest opened. He stood by a great green meadow. Poplar-trees were around it. At its far end was a lake, and by the lake a cow-moose and her calf were feeding. Black shadows of trees were upon the grass, and the sun shone upon the water. Tay John shot the cow-moose and her calf. The people, far back in the forest, heard the noise of his rifle and came running. One by one they escaped the darkness of the trees to stand on the edge of the meadow and rub their eyes that closed against the sunlight. They smelt moose-blood in the air, and shouted to those who were behind to hurry.

The people made their houses by the lake, close to the wall of the forest. They set the doors to face the rising sun, and inside hung mats and made the spruce boughs thick by the sides of the houses where they would sleep. They kindled their fires, laid their fire-tongs and baskets about them. They stayed there, and forgot that they had been on their way to their cousins across the mountains, for now game was around them and the bushes bent with their summer berries.

It had come about as Kwakala said, and Tay John was the leader who had led them and the hunter who had taken the hunger from their bellies. Smutuksen smiled to have seen this before he died.

Of their young men who were old enough yet had not married there were Tay John, Memhaias, and two others, and of their young women there was only one. Her name was Shwat, sister of the raven, daughter of Zohalats, who was the sister of Mingqaias the Liar. After the people had been some time by the lake Shwat came from her shelter beyond the village, where she had been in seclusion that her womanhood might come upon her.

When she was once more among the people, Memhaias, having painted on his back his dream-spirit – an eagle with a spear – went out and looked upon her. He touched her breasts and pointed an arrow against her belly, for these were signs that the girl would understand. He made ready to give her parents presents, and people said that soon there would be a wedding-feast and that Shwat would leave her mother's house to go with Memhaias.

But Tay John looked also upon Shwat. She turned her eyes from him and looked down upon the ground to his shadow, a shadow which no one might touch. She retreated from him, for Memhaias had already spoken, and Tay John with his yellow hair was a leader and not as other men. She was afraid.

Tay John followed. He came close to her. Then, when they were in the middle of the village, where all who were watching might see, he lifted her skirt and ripped open her breech clout – for this, too, was a sign the girl would understand. And Shwat, being still unable to face him and not knowing what to do, ran to her house and stayed there.

That day when darkness was already rising from the ground and people sat about their fires by the house doors, Memhaias met Tay John on the shore of the lake at some distance from the village. They were cousins. They had been friends and learned their hunting together. They had eaten of the same meat and sat by the same fires on the hunting trail, but there was only one woman for two of them.

They were strong men. Their arms and their legs had never been wearied. Their hearts were brave. Neither would let the other see his back.

Memhaias came upon Tay John, and Tay John turned to him. They fought. During the night it stormed. Thunder rolled in the mountains. In the morning women came to the lake for water. They called for people to come down to Tay John and Memhaias, whom they saw far away on the shore.

Hunters said they had seen the ground so torn when two bull moose had fought. Tay John still moved and held his head, bleeding through its yellow hair, by the water to ease it. Memhaias did not move. He was some lengths of a man's body away. One hand clutched grass roots. Grass and willow sticks were clenched in his teeth. His face was blue and soft, like fruit from the hillsides pounded by women for winter food. The people carried him back to the village, bathed him in cold water and beat him with willows till he murmured and his eyes opened. After a while Tay John followed. No one would help him. He was alone.

That night men talked in the village around their fires. Women were indoors, quiet, not moving from the shelter of their houses.

There was no doubt, said Squeleken, that Memhaias had spoken first. The girl was his by the custom of the people, handed down from their fathers. He had done what a man should do. He had painted his body and touched her with an arrow in the belly. He stood ready to make presents to her parents.

Tis-Kwinit spoke. He said: "For all things there is a way. We have our way for our hunting, to bring back meat from the hillsides. We have our way with our women that each man may know he lies with his own and not where another may lie. If the usage of time be not respected, and the mark of a man on a woman mean nothing, then each man must fight for his woman and the fathers of children will be nameless."

Swamas who listened, answered: "We have more young men than we have women," he said. "In these past times when we have hungered mothers have drowned in the rivers their female children that they might not suffer. Are our young men to leave us and go elsewhere to have women?"

Others rose up then to speak. It was true, they said, that there were now more young men than young women among the people. The young men could wait, for after the snow there would be girls, now young, who would reach their womanhood and be ripe for marriage.

One said that the young men should cross over the mountains, make war upon their cousins, and bring women back to the village.

Tzalas spoke. He said only: "Tay John is a leader. He has brought us to this land where we no longer hunger. Other men must marry. The woman of Tay John is the people. He is a leader of the people and is married to their sorrows."

When Tzalas had spoken all were silent, for he alone had not feared to speak the thought in their minds. Only Smutuksen turned from the fireside and walked to his shelter, feeling his way with his stick.

Smutuksen was an old man now, and like Tay John, alone.

Memhaias gave presents to Zohalats and Snikiap, the parents of Shwat. Shwat left her parents and came to his house to live with him, and after she had been there a while her parents returned presents to Memhaias.

In those days, when the snow was yet fresh upon the ground, the people turned and looked for Tay John.

Yet he was not there.

The house where he lived, at the end of the village close to the lake, was empty. Needles had fallen from the spruce boughs so that at noon the sun made the shape of the bare boughs upon the ground in its centre. The ashes of the fire beyond the door had grown cold. Wind blew them away, and the snow covered the place where they had been.

People came by. They stopped. They bent to look in at the door.

The mat where Tay John had slept was there by the wall, but his sleeping-robe was gone, and his rifle, as though he had taken it with him for his hunting.

So they nodded their heads and said, "Yes, he has gone away on his hunting. He has gone into the high mountains, which are still new to our hunters, to find fresh meat and bring it back to the village."

They asked the hunters when they came in if they had seen anything of Tay John, their leader. The hunters said "No"; excepting only one, a young man, who said that he had seen where Tay John had camped high up past the edge of the forest in a place where only the goat would go.

The game up there, the people then said, must be scarce and hard to come upon that he had been gone so long on his hunting. But the young man said "No." "The goats," he said, "are many and easy to kill, for they are strange to the sight of a man."

When the snow grew deep they bent snowshoes out of spruce wood for Tay John to be ready for his feet when he returned. They made him a new house under the ground. Each day they brought fresh boughs, laid them there for his bed, and made a fire against his coming. The young girls, who were not yet of age, with their mothers, fashioned a robe of dark marmot hides, the finest the village had seen. This they hung from the roof, at the wall near the back to be dry from the fire.

Days passed, and they waited.

Smutuksen, whose eyes were fast losing their sight, sat by his fire. He called for Tay John by the old name of Kumkleseem to come to him and touch him in these last days that were his before he died.

"The people now," he said to Kumkleseem, "are your people. They will follow where you lead. They are children. They need a man before them. They must keep to their own ways, and let the white man keep to his."

But Tay John was not there to hear him.

Yet sometimes at night the people would start from their sleep. The men of the village would climb the notched poles to their doors and look out on the snow and the trees and the stars shining bright. A man would say to his neighbour: "It seemed I heard something, as of someone coming. A branch snapped on a tree down yonder by the lake."

And the other would say: "It was the frost, or a moose down from the hill."

They would go back to their robes and their women, and in the morning no one would speak of what had happened during the night.

All that winter smoke rose from the new house built for Tay John. At night an owl perched by it and hooted.

PART TWO

HEARSAY

FIVE

I n the year 1904, and in the years that followed, a new name blew up against the mountains, and an idea stirred like a wind through the valleys.

The name was the name of the new railway, the Grand Trunk Pacific, and the idea was that of a new route to the Pacific – a northern route, bringing the eastern cities, where money bred, closer to the Orient than they had ever been. The smell of Asia was in the air, and men thirsted still for the salt water beyond the mountains.

It would be an imperial route, and in time of war Britain could rush troops across Canada well back from the American border. "It will show these damned Yankees," a Member of Parliament shouted in Ottawa, "that what independence we have we mean to keep."

Out on the prairies the white man's breath had blasted the Indian and the buffalo from the grass lands, now his plough turned the grass under. In small towns, set in half-circles of worship round railway stations, under a sun that laboured across the sky all day, and set at the day's end, great and red and bloated, as though slowly consumed by the fire of its own creating – farmers and settlers and ranchers met. "The Grand Trunk Pacific," they said, "will break the monopoly of the Canadian Pacific. It will bring our freight-rates down. It will give our country back to those who are its rightful owners."

The snow-topped mountains, seen from the plains like the tents of giants pitched to contend man's westward way, would be pierced again. Man would find a pass, lay his rails, and send his trains roaring down to meet the tides. There was Pine Pass, and there was the pass at the head of the Wapiti – but these were far north, close to the tight white line of the Arctic.

Yet if a man looked west from Edmonton, where the forest of the foothill steps upon the plain, to Prince George beyond the first range of the mountains, and beyond that again to the Pacific shore, Yellowhead Pass was in the path of his vision. It was a low pass. Its contours were gentle. It was a gateway opening to the west.

Still, in those days, no man knew. Surveys were sent out to find the way, to besiege the fortress of the mountains, to follow rivers and to pause by lakes, set like moats below rocky walls. Men saw themselves cast in strange shapes by their shadows flung upon untutored ground. They felt the hot breath on their shoulders of those who would come after, with steel rails for the valleys, bridges for the rivers, and ploughs for the fields, and houses for the new clearings in the forest. They shouted words back and went on.

They went on till the hills and peaks closed after them, and behind they saw only what waited ahead. They went on so far into troubled and unearthly land that they wondered, some of those who were young, that their shadows still were with them. They were men carried on the wind of an idea. They found themselves blown up a canyon where man had never been and words never lived before. Nameless river water tugged their saddle stirrups. In the winter silence was about them on the snow like a name each had heard whispered in his mother's womb.

One man who had been out to the country of Yellowhead Pass came back to Edmonton in the days when the railway had been pushed well into the mountains, with a tale. He was a lanky man in his forties, who seemed older. He kept his brown beard tightly clipped. Pouches hung heavily beneath his eyes so that the red of his lower eyelids showed, and someone said of him once, seeing him in his old tweed suit, that he resembled a somewhat thoughtful Saint Bernard dog. He walked along the wooden sidewalks, taller than average, a slouch hat over his eyes, moving at leisure through the world with a long careful stride, appearing to take a step just once in a while.

His name was Jack Denham, but he was known generally as Jackie – a man whose pride was in his past, of which he seldom spoke, but over which loomed the shadow of a great white house in the north of Ireland, in the county of Tyrone. From that past, and because of it, he received four times a year a remittance. Then, in funds, he put up at the Selkirk – Edmonton's first hotel – lived and dined in the style of which the town was capable. His remittance gone, he would be no more seen for a time. He would return to cheap lodgings across the Saskatchewan river, where he cooked his own meals in an unplastered room. He often hired out with outfits going west to the mountains, or north to the Peace. He was a good man with horses and on the river, and once had made a long trip alone by canoe along the north fork of the Peace to its source up against the Arctic Circle. He said he knew the valleys of the mountains and the way the rivers ran better than he knew the lines on the wide, calloused palm of his hand.

He owed money no longer than it took him to make it on the trail. He accepted no drink at the bar unless he could return it. He treated others with no more respect than he regarded as due to himself in turn. Coming back from his journeys to the foothills and the mountains, from that country where words were too often outdistanced by the actions which gave them rise, he was heard with tolerance and interest – one who had held his own in the places he spoke of, whose speech and life were close to events.

All his years in the west, Jack Denham had lived in the midst of events. Yet they had somehow passed him by. He had not given them their shape, and they left him apparently only the man he had always been. He had gone into the Yellowhead country with a survey party scouting a route for the new railway, to swing an axe or handle the rod before the transit of the engineer. To the mountains he had returned to see the rails put down. Up there, he said, at one time only the width of a mountain stream kept him from the adventure of his life.

He would talk about it anywhere – in a pause during dinner at the hotel. He would allude to it suddenly at the bar among strangers over the second glass of whisky. Two tall pale glasses of whisky were his limit. One drink of whisky was good for you, two were too many, three were not enough. "I always take too many," he explained with a laugh and a wide gesture.

He might meet a friend at the street corner and follow him to his destination, talking, stretching his story the length of Edmonton. It became known as "Jackie's Tale." It was a faith – a gospel to be spread, that tale, and he was its only apostle. Men winked over it, smiled at it, yet listened to its measured voice, attentions caught, imaginations cradled in a web of words.

"I almost had an adventure there," Jack Denham would

burst forth, referring to the mountain stream, drawing his chin down against his shoulder, jutting out his lower lip and running his fingers over his soft, fur-like beard.

Do you see what I mean? (the tale continued.) An adventure. A real one. Blood in it. It was a close call. I would have been in on it too, but there was the creek in the way . . . and a man besides.

It would have taken courage to cross that creek. I don't think it was possible to cross. I don't know now. Hard to tell. At the time, anyway, it was impossible. It wasn't wide. Twice as wide as a man, standing, might jump perhaps, but deep and swift. Boiling. There were rapids. That creek – it was white. It was jagged. It had teeth in it. I felt it would have cut me in two. I would have hesitated even with a horse . . . and I was afoot.

And what I saw was worth more than what I would have done. What would I have done had I been on the other side of the creek? That's what I don't know. That's what no man would know, unless he knew what he had always done and could see himself as clearly as I saw that other man across the water from me. But he knew. At least he had no doubts – this other man. No doubts about himself. And there was no doubt about what he saw before him, or, for that matter, about that river at his back. He could no more have forded the river than I, and he had no time. It was a matter of moments, I tell you; split seconds. It was the stuff of a nightmare come alive in broad daylight and throwing its shadow on the ground before you.

Do you see? No matter – for him, for this other man I mean, it must have seemed like a nightmare. Yet I doubt if he, a man of his type, would ever have had a nightmare in his life. No, his sleep would be sleep – just sleep – like a deep shadow between each of his days. Nothing more than that. No place of visions. No birth of creatures to stay with him when he woke and stand between him and the sun. With me it was different. I was an onlooker. I saw what he didn't see. I saw him, for instance. Still, he was aware, it appears to me now, long before I, that something waited for him, although his back was towards it.

You see, I had gone up that valley alone, on foot. It was Sunday, and I left the three of them in camp: Burstall, the boss; Hank, the horse wrangler – we had twelve head of horses with us – and Sam, the cook. We were well up into the mountains, and were on one of the rivers, the Snake Indian. It flows into the Athabaska. There were any number of passes there, and any number of unnamed streams. It is a good game country, too, and on the alplands I could see caribou and flocks of mountain sheep. I had my glasses with me, so that I could have a good look at the high country, also a revolver – only a twenty-two – on the chance of knocking over a few grouse. It was a busman's holiday for me, a walk. It was nothing unusual for us to walk twenty miles in a working day – but here was this valley, with no name, a clear flow of water, clear and cold as spring water, coming from it through a lane of spruce-trees by our camp, and I wanted to see where it led to. A new mountain valley leads a man on like that – like a woman he has never touched.

His experience tells him it will be much like others he knows – a canyon to go through, a meadowland or two, some forest, and its head up against a mountain wall or trickling from a grimy glacier. Yet still he goes up it hoping vaguely for some revelation, something he has never seen or felt before, and he rounds a point or pushes his head over a pass, feeling that a second before, that had he come a second earlier, he would have surprised the Creator at his work – for a country where no man has stepped before is new in the real sense of the word, as though it had just been made, and when you turn your back upon it you feel that it may drop back again into the dusk that gave it being. It is only your vision that holds it in the known and created world. It is physically exhausting to look on unnamed country. A name is the magic to keep it within the horizons. Put a name to it, put it on a map, and you've got it. The unnamed – it is the darkness unveiled. Up in those high places you even think you can *hear* the world being made. Anyway you can hear the silence, which is the sound of the earth's turning, or time going by.

At any rate I had gone up this river, or creek, or whatever you want to call it, and its valley had surprised me. It was tight and narrow all the way. A canyon at first where I had some pretty rock climbing to do. After that a long belt of forest. Near the end of this forest belt I found a dead tree that spanned the stream and crossed to the other side where the going appeared better. There was no sign of man up there at all – no old stumps, no blazes – nothing. Beside the caribou and sheep far above the timber I saw not a living thing – not a squirrel, nor a mouse, nor a humming fly. I came almost to the headwaters where a great green glacier moved down, when I turned around to reach camp before dark. It got on my nerves a bit, I guess, that river, being penned up with it all day long and having its roar in my head. It filled my head, my thoughts. It was enough to make me stagger. I crossed the river again on the dead tree, and about two miles below that tree and about the same distance above the canyon through which the river broke out into the main valley where we had our camp, I stopped to have a smoke and to look up a side valley coming down from the north. A stream came in from the north across from me and spread in shallows over a gravel flat.

Tall green grass grew there on a sort of island, and behind was the forest leading up a narrow valley between two towering mountains. Somewhere up there I remember was a waterfall. I could see it, but, though it was quite close, a long white line against the rock, the sound of its fall was drowned by the river before me. As I say, it wasn't wide, that river I was following. Twice as wide as a man might jump, perhaps, but it was swift, and I could hear the boulders rolling in the surge of its waters.

Then across from me, as though he had grown there while my eyes blinked, I saw a man. He was stripped to the waist, wearing only moccasins and a pair of moose-hide leggings. Behind him some little distance I saw his rifle stacked against a tree and beside it his pack with a shirt of caribou hide, the hair still upon it, tossed upon the ground. He had come down the creek opposite me. What he was doing there when I saw him, standing out on that flat among the grasses, I don't know. About to make his camp for the night perhaps.

Anyway, he saw me. He doubtless saw me before I saw him. He would have, that sort of fellow. He looked at me, yet gave no sign of recognition. He was tall, dark of skin as an Indian, yet his hair was full and thick and yellow, and fell low to his shoulders. His eyes were black, and I was so close to him that I could see their whites, and his nostrils flex ever so slightly and his white teeth showed when he breathed. From behind me the shadows of the trees were reaching across the water, but he stood full in the sun. His brown skin glowed, and his muscles were a pattern of shadows across his chest and belly. He had a build, that fellow. Still, there was something, it is hard to say, something of the abstract about him – as though he were a symbol of some sort or other. He seemed to stand for something. He stood there with his feet planted apart upon the ground, as though he owned it, as though he grasped it with them. When he moved I would not have been surprised to have seen clumps of earth adhere to the soles of his moccasins and the long shadows of his muscles across his body – they weren't strength in the usual sense of being able to lift weights and that kind of thing. They represented strength in the abstract. Endurance, solitude – qualities that men search for. It was in his face, too, long and keen as though shaped by the wind, and beardless as a boy's – those fellows – I could see he was of mixed blood – are often lightly bearded. I felt I was an intruder, and could I have spoken to him I believe I would have tried to excuse my presence there, along the lonely river.

But I couldn't speak to him. There was too much noise with that confounded water. I shouted. "Hallo!" I shouted; "Hallo!" I waved my arms and shouted again. It seemed absurd. I was so close to him that he should have been able to hear a whisper. He stood there across from me, too, with his head tilted a bit as though he were listening. Yet even then it seemed he wasn't listening to me at all, but to something else I couldn't hear. Had he been able to hear me, for all I knew then, he wouldn't have understood what I said. But, still, he wasn't all Indian. There was that yellow hair. It was long and heavy. A girl would have been proud of it, and he had it held with some sort of a band around his forehead. A black band, like a strip of hide cut from some small fur-bearing animal. A piece of marten, say.

Yes, his hair shone. It seemed to shed a light about him. Then he looked directly at me. I was still gesturing, throwing my arms about, trying to draw attention to myself. In short, making a very vulgar display. He looked as though he thought so, anyway. My arms dropped to my side. I tell you, I was ashamed. I have no doubt he would have spoken to me had we met in the usual way. But here was this rushing torrent between us. We couldn't cross it. Our voices couldn't be heard above it. He accepted that for the impossibility it was, while I was making frantic efforts at evasion. When he looked at me I could see the reflected light of the sun burning deep down in his dark eyes. Then he turned slowly, as if in disgust at what he saw, and took a step back towards his rifle.

And in that moment, while his foot was lifted for his second step, and his back towards me, it happened. Suddenly it seemed to me like a play being put on for my benefit, with the forest and mountains for backdrop, the gravel bar where this Yellowhead was for stage, and the deep river with its unceasing crescendo for the orchestra pit.

A bear was there above him, between him and his rifle. It may have been there for some time. Anyway it was there now, no question about it. A grizzly bear at that, a silver tip, with a great roll of muscle over its shoulders and the hair slowly rising in fear along the length of its backbone. For the bear was frightened, make no mistake about that. Later when it stood up I saw it was a she-bear. She probably had a cub cached somewhere close by. As a rule, of course, a bear won't attack a man – but this was a she-grizzly, and she was trapped. There was the pack behind her, you see, with its human smell. There was the man before her. Her cub was somewhere near by. If she hadn't been frightened or angered – and the cause and often the result of the one is much the same as the other – she would have turned around and left a situation she was unprepared to meet. But, no, she stood her ground.

And my Yellowhead across from me stood his. He slowly, ever so slowly, put his foot back upon the ground and waited. He stood, a bronze and golden statue planted among the grasses that rose up to his knees. This was the sort of thing I had some-times dreamed of – of meeting a bear one day close up, hand to hand so to speak, and doing it in. An epic battle: man against the wilderness. And now I saw the battle taking form, but another man was in my place and with the river between us I could give no help. None at all. My revolver? I might have hit the man, but against the bear it was worth no more than shooting peas. I waited.

Something was going to happen. The grizzly opened her mouth. I saw her sharp white teeth. She flicked the grass with her long-nailed fore-paw. That paw seemed suddenly to sprout out from her body, then to be drawn back. She advanced a step. I saw the right hand of this Yellowhead fellow move gently to his waist and come out with the handle of a gleaming knife in its fist. The muscles along his shoulders rippled. His rifle was beyond his reach, past the bear. He glanced not once at the river nor at me behind him. His eyes I knew were on the bear. She swung her head low, from side to side, as though she cautioned him to be careful. Her mouth opened and she roared. I could hear that across the river. It came to me faintly, like a cough.

Then Yellowhead moved quickly. His left hand swiped the band off his head and threw it towards the grizzly, not directly at her, but just above her head. She reared up, and then I saw the hang of her laden teats. She stood so that she towered above Yellowhead. That's what I called him now. I found myself saying "Yellowhead," "Yellowhead." I had to give him a name so that I could help him – morally, you know. I had to align him with the human race. Without a name no man is an individual, no individual wholly a man.

There she was above him, immense and unassailable as a mountain side. She clawed the air after this black thing that flew towards her. And when she swung he sprang beneath her arm. I saw his left hand grab the long fur around her neck, and

I saw his right swing twice with the long-bladed knife, and the knife stayed there the second time, a flash of light embedded in her side, searching for the great, slow beat of her heart. It was a matter of moments. Then they were on the ground rolling over and over. I caught glimpses now and then of that yellow mass of hair, like a bundle the she-grizzly held with affection to her breast. It was his only chance. If he had stepped back from her those claws would have ripped his belly open, torn his head from off his shoulders. He did the one thing, the only thing he could have done, and did it well.

They rolled to the very edge of the stream on whose other bank I stood. They were quiet there. Yellowhead was beneath. "If he's not dead," I said, "he's drowned." The great mass of fur was quiescent before me, and from its side a stream of dark blood flowed into the hungry river.

Then the mass quivered. It heaved. A man's head appeared beside it, bloody, muddied, as though he were just being born, as though he were climbing out of the ground. Certainly man had been created anew before my eyes. Like birth itself it was a struggle against the powers of darkness, and Man had won. Like birth, too, it was a cry and a protest – his lips parted as though a cry, unheard by me, came from them. Death, now that is silence – an acceptance – but across this creek from me was life again. Man had won against the wilderness, the unknown, the strength that is not so much beyond our strength as it is capable of a fury and single passion beyond our understanding. He had won. *We* had won. That was how I felt. I shouted. I did a dance. Then I calmed down. I wanted more than anything I knew to go across and touch this man, this Yellowhead, to tell him, "Well done!" But I couldn't cross that river. I might have gone back to the foot log, but that would have taken more than an hour, and it would seem that I was leaving him in his moment of victory – when no man wishes to be alone. A victory is no victory until it has been shared. Defeat? Well, that is another matter.

But Yellowhead was damaged. Somehow the grizzly had clawed his face. One side of it streamed blood. It looked raw like meat. For a time he sat there on the ground, among the grasses, and the blood ran off his shoulder, down his arm, down between his very fingers. He didn't look at me. Seemed to have forgotten all about me. He stared with wonder, I think, at the body of the bear lying half in the river. He spat some of her fur out, caught between his teeth. Then he washed his face, found the band for his hair and bound it back. After that he took his knife, still caught between the she-grizzly's ribs, cut her head off, neatly severing the vertebrae at its base, climbed with it up a tree and left it there, caught in a crotch so that it gazed upon the scene of its dismay.

He came down to the side of the river, bathed his face again. It still bled. I shouted, but he didn't hear me, or didn't care to. He disdained me, that fellow, absolutely.

It was growing dusk now. He went back to the edge of the forest where his pack and rifle rested. He staggered once and leaned against a tree. Then he pulled on his caribou-hide shirt, hoisted his pack and shouldered it. He picked up his rifle and stepped, without one backward glance, behind the trees. He vanished, as though he were leaving one form of existence for another. For a moment or two I saw his yellow head, a gleam of light being carried away through the timber. He had come down from the high country to do his job, and having done it, left. Entering the forest his pack brushed against a branch of spruce. The branch moved there before my eyes, swayed gently, touched by an invisible hand after he had gone. It moved. The river flowed. The headless trunk of the she-grizzly swung out a bit from the bank, rolled over in the force of the current, as if in her deep sleep she dreamed. Night's shadow was on the valley. Trees creaked in a new wind blowing. An owl hooted somewhere close to me.

It was late when I got back to camp. It was dark, black as the inside of a bear. Night was about me like a covering from which I tried to escape. My hands wandered far from me feeling my way. My fingers touched branches, the harsh bark of trees. I pulled them back to me, held them against my sides. They were some company for me in the darkness.

Days passed before I told them in the camp of what I had seen on the banks of the river that streamed clear and fresh and nameless before our tents. It took me a time to find the words.

If there had been a glass of whisky – whisky, another victory of man against the powers of darkness, whatever they may be.

SIX

It was early autumn, you see, when I saw this grizzly fight. Yes, it was quite early – in September probably, although out there it's only the seasons and not the months that are important. Still, on that survey we were aware of time. We worked feverishly, sixteen hours a day when the days were long. You would have thought someone was treading on our heels the way we ran through those mountains to see all that we could see. And, of course, someone was. People were there behind us, impatient, waiting; the railway men armed with their axes and picks and shovels and gunpowder, ready to do war against the mountains when, with the reports from our party and others like us, they could map their campaign.

It was early autumn, then, before the snow began to fly. – (There's an expression for you, born in the country, born from the imaginations of men and their feeling for the right word, the only word, to mirror clearly what they see! Those with few words must know how to use them.) Men who have seen it, who have watched it day by day outside their cabin window coming down from the sky, like the visible remorse of an ageing year; who have watched it bead upon the ears of the horses they rode, muffle the sound of hoofs on the trail, lie upon spruce boughs and over grass – cover, as if for ever, the landscape in which they moved, round off the mountains, blanket the ice on the rivers – for them, the snow flies. The snow doesn't fall. It may ride the wind. It may descend slowly, in utter quiet, from the grey and laden clouds, so that you can hear the flakes touching lightly on the wide white waste, as they come to rest at the end of their flight. Flight – that's the word. They beat in the air like wings, as if reluctant ever to touch the ground. I have observed them coming down, on a very cold day, near its end when the sky above me was still blue, in flakes great and wide as the palm of my hand. They were like immense moths winging down in the twilight, making the silence about me visible.

And we were out in it all that winter, in the snow and silence, Burstall and myself, travelling through the country on snow-shoes, with packs and a canvas lean-to on our backs, mapping, following rivers to their heads.

We had sent our horses with Hank and Sam, the wrangler and cook, back to the foothills before the freeze-up. We were to meet again in the spring on Solomon's Flats, on the edge of the foothills, where Colin McLeod had his trading post, and go on with our work. That was when I took up with this Yellowhead again – or rather at first with what you might call the remnants of his presence.

Solomon's Flats? Well, Solomon's Flats are that rare thing in the mountains, a wide, flat place, a sort of prairie-land of grass and flowers, studded with clumps of willow and shadowed with poplars. They say they got this name from an old Indian chief who hunted there many years ago. It is a place where men for more than a hundred years, travelling into the mountains, have stopped to rest their horses. It is pocked with old camp-fire circles. Solomon creek flows by its east side below Solomon mountain into the wide, grey Athabaska, beyond which spruce-trees stand like men with lances limned against the sky. Solomon mountain is not really a mountain at all. They call it that because it overtops all the other foothills around it. In the summer, red and blue and yellow flowers grow upon its slopes, and heavy grass hangs there where deer used to feed. In the summer an occasional moose beds down under the poplars gathered in the draws.

Solomon mountain looks across the flats to the first range of the Rockies. At times over those flats white clouds drift, rimmed in gold, above the earth, above its darkness, above the lantern glow of the cabin and the fires men have kindled in the open. Again, the northern lights appear across a cloudless sky like banners of a god-like host borne on a soundless wind.

We came down there in the spring, when the snow was still in the high mountains. We came down into green grass and leaves. We took our snowshoes off and slung them on our backs up on a sunny side-hill. We stepped off the snow on to the ground. I was so glad to feel the soft, moist earth, warmed ever so little by the sun, against my moccasin soles that I leaned down and put a bit of it between my lips and sucked it. It tasted sweet.

Colin McLeod was there by his trader's cabin, and we were pleased to see him. He stood out there in the sunlight awaiting our approach. We had shouted from far back. Out there you don't go up to a man's door and knock upon it. Oh, no! If you did, you might be met with the muzzle of a rifle. You would startle the man inside who at best sees the wilderness around him as an enemy.

McLeod stood out there and waited, his hands upon his hips. He was a small Scotsman, with bow legs, a red bristle of beard, and small quick blue eyes, so constantly shifting, I thought he might be looking for a place to hide. As we approached, he took a blue handkerchief from his pocket and began to polish his bald (and tanned) head. There was a touch of anxiety in the movement, as though he sweated, as though he feared we walked in peril and might never get to him at all. Still it was only a gesture and I got to know it well. I have to say, however, that he did a good job with his polishing. The dome of his head was burnished. It was like a piece of old, well-seasoned oak, weathered with the seasons.

He had built his cabin there himself on the flats some half-mile back from the Athabaska, in a grove of spruce where a channel of the Solomon gushed from the ground in a spring and gave him water. He was in what you might call a strategic position as a fur trader, close to the main trail through the mountains and foothills to Edmonton, and on Solomon creek where bands of dark-skinned hill people, descendants of Crees and of French-Canadian and Iriquois *voyageurs* of the early days, rode in each spring from their hunting grounds at Grande Cache, more than a hundred miles west on the Smokey River, to barter their winter's catch for firearms, woollen shirts, bright silk handkerchiefs, beads, flour, tea, and vanilla extract which they drank to drunkenness. In short, for anything he had – eager to be rid of their possessions at any cost. He had made money from his trading, taking his furs into town himself, or sending them with someone who was going that way.

His cabin was small, of spruce logs chinked with white clay from the river bank, its doorway facing up the Solomon, guarding the trade route. In the front room was a small counter and behind it shelves with his goods. Great barrels, hooped with maple, held flour and sugar and dried fruit. Behind the counter was his bedroom where he lived and cooked his meals. He had a fireplace in there, in a corner, built of coloured field stones, and his bed, red Hudson's Bay blankets tossed upon it. Before the fireplace a great round butt of a spruce log served as a table, and he had made chairs from box-boards and stout limbs of willow steamed and twisted into fantastic shapes. At the head of the bed, tacked above it on the wall, was a large print of a girl, veiled in mists of modesty, who was always about to step into a fresh and bubbling pool, by whose sides the grass was forever green, the trees eternally in leaf, and the sky above steadfastly blue.

McLeod led us into that back room and filled our bellies with food. He and Burstall had met before, and after the meal I listened, half drowsing, to their talk. Another party, it seemed, had passed through there before us, with horses, on their way out from up the Athabaska. This was in May, and the country in the lower valleys had been open for some time. There had been a man with them by the name of Timberlake whom Burstall had wanted to see. We both knew him. While I listened I heard the name of Tay John mentioned more than once.

"Tay John," I said. "Who is he? What does he do?"

McLeod described him to me.

"That's the man I saw," I said, "up a creek fighting a grizzly bear." I told him what I had seen.

"So you know him?" I asked.

"Know him?" McLeod rose, pushed the dishes back from the table top and pointed to some dark stains in the wood. "Know him?" His stubby forefinger cushioned itself on the table underneath our noses.

"Look at that – what do you make of that?" he said.

I looked closer. "Blood, perhaps. I don't know." It was a great wandering black stain, like the map of Russia.

"Blood. You're right, man, that's what it is. And I can't wash it off. I've scrubbed and soaped and still there it is, and I have to eat off it. It's on the floor, too. Blood on the floor. I tell you a while ago, this place stank with it. Stank. That's the word."

He began again the rhythmic polishing of his bald head with the blue handkerchief. It seems that Tay John had left the flats shortly before our arrival, on horseback. He had arrived afoot, with furs to trade, and went away on horseback, on Timberlake's favourite saddle-mare.

"Sure, I remember her," Burstall said, "a fine tall sorrel with a white stocking on her forefoot. We came into the mountains last summer across the river from here with Timberlake and his party. Yes, he was proud of the mare. She was too good a horse for trail work."

According to McLeod, Timberlake had wintered on Henry House Flats with his horses, some miles up the Athabaska, and had camped on Solomon Flats for some days on his way out to give his horses a good feed of grass, as good as they could get on the new grass only half an inch above the ground. While they were camped there, close to McLeod's cabin, this Yellowhead, or Tay John fellow, arrived from up the Solomon with his furs.

He had been in that part of the mountains for some time, for three years or more, and McLeod was glad to take his furs which were always prime. "He has a feeling for fur," McLeod said. "He seems to know where to go to find marten darker than any I have ever seen before. He comes down here with a hundred pounds of fur on his back and dumps it at my door and stands back, proud as . . . well, proud as a chief."

And it appears that some sort of a chief was exactly what Tay John was. He wasn't Cree, McLeod said. Couldn't even speak their language, although his English was as good as a man could expect. How he had learned it – well, I asked McLeod that. He said Tay John told him once that from his Indian village to the west of the mountains when he was little more than a boy he had gone out with prospectors' parties – and others as well. Also he was curious in a general way, and at McLeod's cabin passed hours looking through old catalogues and magazines, puzzling out the words, bringing a page up to McLeod and asking about something he couldn't quite understand. There were pictures, you see, of rifles and so on, and that helped him some. McLeod had a Bible there. Tay John had folded its covers about his ears. He spoke slowly, but he knew how to use his words. He was a Shuswap. Why he had left his people, he never said. "Mixed blood," McLeod said. "Something working in the man. You can feel it when he is around. There's some sort of a story, too, a legend if you want to call it so, that he was to be a great leader among them and that he ran out and left them. I wouldn't ask him, because he wouldn't tell me, but it's in his bearing, in just the way he carries himself. For one thing when he comes down here, he stands on the edge of the clearing and waits for me to come out and bring him over to the door. He never calls. He may be there hours sometimes, waiting, for all I know. But he always waits until his presence is recognised."

Anyway, it was apparent that, at least until this last affair, a friendship had developed between McLeod and Tay John. Tay John had found an old cabin back in the mountains, abandoned by the trapper who had built it, where he made his headquarters and from there at intervals, even during the winter, he would come down to visit McLeod. He was a man who had left the world he knew, the world of his own people, and moved now on the rim of the white man's world forming around him. He might never be able to enter it, but he was drawn to it, as the wild fowl are drawn to their flocks upon the breeding waters.

Yes, there was that in it, too. McLeod brought us over to the picture of the girl hung above his bed. "Look at that," he said, "those smudges. He stands in front of that sometimes, saying nothing, just staring, and runs his fingers over it." I could see the grimy marks of fingers where they had touched the shape of breasts and the curve of thighs.

I gathered from what I heard that once in a while Tay John and McLeod had even had a drink or two together. At times with the lantern hanging above them they sat down before the fireplace and played a hand of cards, anything to pass the long winter hours in that wind-battered cabin.

There they were, the two of them, the short, bald-headed Scotsman, whose life was work and scheming, the chasing of the almighty dollar, and Tay John, the young man, born to be a leader among his own kind, who had turned from his fortune as another man might turn and walk out of the door of his house, and who, if he thought of it at all, perhaps thought that now he was a man unknown, the stream of whose life no longer flowed clear and sure, walled no longer by the faith of his people, but dammed into a pool and wasting its waters in muskegs and shallows.

To me he was still the man on the lonely creek who had outfought the grizzly bear. After all, we know a man only by what has happened to him. He was for me cast in an heroic mould. That there was some shadow of a past, some hint of a destiny he had forsaken, that had forsaken him, made him stand the taller and his yellow hair to shine the brighter. No, not like a halo. Halos after all are tailor-made, and, if you notice, always worn at a rakish angle. No, it was more like a torch, that hair, it seemed to me – a flame, anyway, to light the hopes of his people, whatever they may have been.

Tay John came down with his furs from the mountains in the spring, before we reached the flats. McLeod went out to meet him and brought him over to the cabin. It was late in the day. Shadows were long upon the ground, and in the air was the smell of wood smoke and of food cooking from outside Timberlake's tents beyond the spruce-trees. A shaft of the sun came low through the branches of the trees and lay upon a grassy mound rising just beyond the cabin door. Tay John lifted his furs from his back, unpacked them and spread them there. He placed his marten skins with their fine dark furs above the others. Two black wolves and three pelts of lynx he laid below them, and upon the wolf hides six slim white skins of weasels – those white arrows of death. He was a showman in his way, and stood back and looked upon what he had brought down from the mountains, glowing there before him in the day's last light, brown and grey and golden, white as snow, dark as nameless river water.

McLeod said, "Gold from the forest, eh?"

Two other men had come out from the cabin with him, tall men in high-heeled riding boots with wide-brimmed hats on their heads, who stood silent, watching. One of them took the cigarette from his mouth and spat.

"Good fur," Tay John said.

I had all this, of course, from McLeod, who stepped forward then, lifted one of the marten skins, shook the fur down and ran his fingers through it. "Looks pretty good," he said – he was no man to commit himself – "We'll go over it in the morning."

While they waited there another man rode up, Timberlake on his sorrel mare. He is an odd-looking fellow. A long time ago he lost an eye. But the other eye from under his black hat, pulled low to hide his hurt, stares out upon the world, calm and level and brooding, like an eye along a rifle-barrel. He is thin and wiry, quick in his movements as a squirrel – a dark man, not too tall, with a long nose and that one eye, half sinister, until you get to know him for what he is. He dismounted, dropped his lines and joined the group around the furs.

"Hm . . . a nice catch," he said. "Whose are they – yours?"

Tay John murmured. He made a movement of his head that might have been assent or denial. His eyes had left the furs and were on the saddle mare, the tall sorrel with cream-coloured mane and tail. Her hooves were small. She had clean legs, with a white stocking on the near forefoot, a deep chest and the saddle sat well upon her withers. She was long muscled, and strong winded. She stood there in the new green grass, her haunch touched and her flank shadowed by the fading sunlight. Tay John looked upon her, and I suppose saw her as more than a horse. She would raise him above the ground and his feet would no longer be the servants of rocky trails. It seemed he wanted her with his hands, his feet, with all of him. He saw himself, felt himself, the movement and the smell of horse, sweat and all, riding through the mountains on that sorrel mare. Perhaps he remembered his village, where he came from beyond the mountains – and he returning with a horse beneath him. The Shuswaps, so far as I know, are not horsemen. On this horse he would be lifted above the others. They would look up to him. He saw the upturned faces. He stepped over the grass to touch the mare.

She snorted, and there in the twilight roses bloomed in her nostrils.

Timberlake jumped around. "Don't go near that mare. She's touchy with strangers."

Tay John, standing, his fingers laced into her mane as though to assert his claim, said he wanted the horse for his own. He said, "Yes, I will take *her*, and you" – he pointed to his furs laid out upon the grassy mound – "you take my furs."

McLeod began to polish that brown round head of his. "He means that he'll trade you his furs for the mare," he said.

"But I need the mare . . . and those furs . . . what are they worth anyway?"

"Oh, quite a bit." McLeod said. "I can't just say now. We're going over them in the morning. But quite a bit, you can be sure of that!"

By the fireplace that night, in McLeod's back room after supper, Timberlake said, "Besides, I'm no fur-trader. What could I do with a lot of furs?"

"Sell them, I suppose," McLeod said. "You couldn't wear them very well. Not all of them, anyway."

McLeod found himself supporting Tay John, trying to trade off the furs, a part of the business on which he himself depended for his living, for the sorrel mare. He told me he did it . . . oh, he didn't know why he did it, except perhaps that it was his nature to be interested in a bargain, any sort of a bargain, for he saw life only as a series of trades. Besides he was aware that for Tay John, for whom he had a feeling, a sympathy, a respect, this was no ordinary matter, that the horse meant more to him than it ever could to Timberlake. Also Tay John might have stolen the horse while she was turned loose at night to graze and ridden off into the hills. Still he was not a man to steal. He wore his hair too long.

Timberlake sat there for a long time smoking his pipe before the fire, his one eye glowing like a live coal far back under his brow.

"Well, I don't think I want to do anything about it," he said finally.

"Why not do this – play a game of cards . . . and settle it." McLeod glanced up at Tay John, standing by the doorway, arms folded, gazing into the fire, the red scar of the grizzly claws still discernible, crawling down his left cheek to below his ear.

"How about it, Tay John?" Tay John smiled. His teeth gleamed white for a moment. He nodded several times slowly.

Timberlake said, "You mean to play with the horse and the furs as stakes?"

McLeod assented.

"But two men can't play poker."

"Cut the cards, then."

"One cut?"

"Aye, one cut. Tay John's furs against your sorrel mare."

That's what they decided on finally. Timberlake had all the best of the bargain. The furs represented one man's whole winter of work. They were worth three sorrel mares and more.

"We'll make this an occasion!" McLeod was up and out of the room. He returned with a bottle of rum which he put on the spruce-butt that was the table. He went outside again and came back with a new log for the fire, swung from the blade of his heavy double-bitted axe. New shadows danced in the room, and for a time the lantern hanging above was dimmed in the blaze from the chimney corner. Tay John and Timberlake sat across from one another, the table low as their knees, while Timberlake's two men stood behind him observing. Later on he was to be glad they were there. McLeod sat between the players, facing the fireplace. A red handkerchief bound Tay John's head. He waited for the cards, immobile as – well, immobile as an idol. Timberlake ran his fingers quickly through his thin black hair, as though he wished to tear it from his scalp. His lonely eye blinked once.

McLeod shuffled the cards.

The bottle of rum passed around.

Timberlake brushed the back of his hand across his lips and said, "Tay John cuts first. All his furs against my riding mare."

Tay John cut. He turned up the jack of spades.

It was a pretty good card. I guess he considered it so, too. The name of the mare was written on it. He thought of her out on the flats nibbling grass beneath the stars. His horse, on which he would ride to his destiny like a warrior to the wars. In the dim light I dare say he could see the picture of that white-skinned girl above the head of McLeod's bed. That was something else he wanted, also, and with a horse beneath him and a road before him . . . who knows?

Timberlake's nostrils, thin as parchment, tightened. Of course, for him, it was nothing so much. There were other horses in his outfit. He wasn't afoot in a strange world in the sense that Tay John was.

He cut. His hand withdrawn revealed the queen of hearts. He had won by one card. He had the white-skinned woman on his side.

Tay John was back on the ground again.

He glanced over at Timberlake.

"You win, eh?" he said.

Timberlake agreed. "I win, Tay John."

Tay John said, "I have my rifle – still."

"A rifle?"

"My rifle and my beaded buckskin shirt?" Tay John had nothing else – nothing at all in the whole wide world.

"No interest. You've lost."

McLeod said, "Yes, I guess you've lost, Tay John."

Tay John reached for the bottle and took a long drink. What's that Jack London, the writer fellow, said about liquor setting the maggots to crawl in your head? Something of the sort, anyway. You know how the third drink will go through you sometimes like a shout in a dead white silence. It's the echoes that seem to crawl, yes, maggot-like, into your being, until your thoughts, if you have any, stir like old leaves.

They sat still some moments yet around that table. Outside the wind moved with sorrow through the trees. Someone shuffled his boot on the floor. McLeod drew in his nostrils and sniffed. The flame rose high in the fireplace.

Tay John said, "Wait!" He was pretty drunk, you know – must have been. Give those fellows a drink who have Indian blood in them and you've started something. . . . *Pouff!* Like that. They were all a bit affected, a bit under the influence by this time, I dare say. Trader's rum is stout stuff.

He told them to wait. Then he leaned over, his left hand on the table-top where he had cut the cards, the card still in his fingers, and grasped with his right hand the axe McLeod had left against the wall. He stood up suddenly, and I guess Timberlake and McLeod rose with him, shoving back their chairs, expecting violence. They had it, too, but not the sort they looked for. Tay John, before they could reach him, swung the axe high, its blade gleaming for an instant above his yellow hair, stooped, and brought it down in one clean sweeping blow upon his left wrist resting on the table. McLeod said you could hear the click as it bit through the bone.

"*Jesus!*" Timberlake shouted, knocking his chair over as

he drew back and wiping a hand across his face where blood had spurted from an artery in the severed wrist.

The brown-skinned hand was before them on the table-top, its fingers slowly knuckling as the tendons contracted. It seemed still alive.

Tay John pointed. "'If your hand offend you,'" he quoted, "'cut it off.' There," he said, "there . . . there is something you *have* to take! . . . against your mare!"

He waved the stump of his wrist that spouted blood into the room like a hose. He swung the axe in a wide circle. The sight of blood, his own blood, brought madness into his eyes. They did the only thing they could do.

One of Timberlake's men ducked under the axe-head and put his arms around Tay John's body. The others closed in. They flung him on the bed and held him there while he struggled. "He was strong," McLeod told me. "To get him down was like trying to bend a four-inch spruce to the ground. But we held him. We had to. He would have killed us or died from bleeding unless we held him and I put a tourniquet around his forearm. All the time he was singing some outlandish song in Shuswap. We stayed with him, the four of us, until he wearied. All night – I remember once the lantern went out. I had to fill it and light it again! Tay John's body quivered. He quietened finally, defiant but exhausted."

And all the while that brown hand was there before them on the table-top. It hunched before the dwindling fire in the fireplace like a great bloated spider. No one touched it. They couldn't bring themselves to touch it, and blood flowed from it to the floor. Blood was everywhere anyway – on the log walls, the ceiling, on their clothes, and smeared across their faces.

When Timberlake went away down the valley he left the mare. He wouldn't even take the fur. "No," he said to

McLeod, "a man who wants something as much as he wants that mare . . . well, he deserves to have it." He left her tied to a poplar-tree so that she wouldn't follow the string of pack horses. That was Timberlake's way.

For a time Tay John was downcast. He stayed in the cabin and bathed the stump of his arm in a steaming brew made from spruce needles. He said to McLeod, "Now I am no longer Tay John. Now they will call me The One-Handed."

"There you are," McLeod finished. "One day he was here, the next morning before I was up he had gone, mangled wrist and sorrel mare, with an old saddle I lent him, back into the mountains. His hand . . . oh, he took that somewhere, some place, back into the hills. Buried it, perhaps. I don't know. He'll never use it again anyway, but he asked me for it. Those spots on that table . . . I scrub and I wash. Still they stay there. I think I can taste them in my food. Whenever I see them I think of that night and that man, who was in those moments, anyway, a madman, swinging the stump of his arm around his head as if he were going to drown us all in a bath of blood."

SEVEN

Possession is a great surrender. The more a man has, the more surely is he owned by what he has. Man, the possessor, on this earth runs from servitude to servitude. He seeks to rid himself of one encumbrance only that he may be free to embrace the burden of another. Land, houses, money – he must serve their growth, their numbers, their exactions. Freedom for most of us, brief, evading precise definition, is only the right to seek a further bondage.

Tay John, of course, could hardly be called a man of possessions. Yet he possessed Timberlake's saddle-mare – and no man must be more faithful in his service than a horseman. That he had one horse instead of many made his task the more demanding. For horses – like man, like his possessions – seek their kind.

And from the beginning it would seem the mare set out to introduce Tay John to her own people – to her own world, to bring him back to the low country where in the spring the succulent grass grew, where horses ran in herds, where men under canvas sought a way for the rails into the mountains.

How she succeeded – how she brought him, against his will, washed him up against a strange tent's door – was a story which found its root in the memories of men, and its form, and a sequence to its incidents in their speech.

For your backwoodsman is a thorough gossip. Left alone he gossips to himself. He lives too much with silence to value it unduly. He pays for a meal, for a night's lodging, with a tale. His social function is to hand on what he has heard, with the twist his fancy has been able to add. He deals with things done – and with the shadows and the hopes of things waiting to be done. What he has not seen he deduces, and what he cannot understand he explains.

Each valley where a cabin has been built has its lore kept alive by the unceasing movement of human lips and tongues. And out of that, like smoke from a smudge – and perhaps no more defined – rises sometimes the figure of a man; not of the real man, perhaps, but of the man other men have seen and spoken to. So it was, I suppose, with Tay John and Solomon's Flats and the country behind – and the story of his mare and all the rest. It began with McLeod and Charlie, the red-whiskered trail cook. Unnumbered others took it up and passed it on.

A good day's journey north of McLeod's trading post is a lake – Rock Lake, lying between the foothills and the mountains. To the west, in a pass above it, in the first range of the mountains are two smaller lakes, one draining into Rock Lake and the other south and east into the Athabaska by Moosehorn creek. Between these two lakes, close to the height of land, was the cabin where Tay John lived. When he first came its roof had fallen under the snow, but the walls still stood. He had cleared it out, and inside the walls set up a tepee of moose-hides. It became his headquarters, a place he went out from and came back to, where he kept a few pots and pans, and some traps, got from McLeod.

Up there he brought his mare when, in the late spring which comes to the high country, snow still lay in the hollows, while on the wind-blown ridges a persevering rabbit would have starved to death.

And there by sagacity, by strength, by a cunning to match her own, he kept her for two months or more, though on the upwind in the afternoons came to her nostrils the smell of ripe forage from down below. He turned her loose to graze. If at night she wandered he tracked her, caught her, tied her to a tree, till she was hungry again and would feed rather than travel.

But a horse alone sometimes, though knee-deep in grass, will run himself thin, hunting for his fellows. A herd – a man can ride herd on a bunch of horses, needing only feed to hold them. But a horse alone needs the herd. And Tay John, of course, when his mare was turned loose, as she had to be to feed, was afoot – a man, one-handed, his mangled forearm in a sling.

It was late in July that McLeod saw him, coming at a jog-trot down the trail from the head of the Solomon.

"Did you see the mare?" Tay John asked when they came close.

"The mare? No, I didn't see her."

"She pulled out," Tay John said. "Last night she started down this way." With no further introduction he dropped to his knees, signalling to McLeod to follow. "See!" he pointed. "It's her track. I've followed it down."

"Of course," McLeod said, bending over. "I saw the tracks – but there are often horses through around here. I didn't know the tracks were hers. Are you sure yourself?"

Tay John grinned. "A man always knows the tracks of the horse he rides like he knows his own feet. Come, look here." He beckoned. McLeod crawled after him. It was a bit like a game of marbles. They came to a place where the trail was rocky. Here the mare had left it and found her way through the spruce thicket.

"She is barefoot," explained Tay John, "and her feet are tender."

"Come to think of it, I did hear a horse go by the cabin last night," McLeod said.

"And you didn't stop her? You didn't go out to catch her?"

"How could I? It was dark – well, I would have gone out if I had thought. But I figured she would stay around until the morning – the feed's so good there. Besides, I didn't know it was Timberlake's mare."

"Not Timberlake's. Mine." Tay John, risen to his feet, tapped his chest. He was gaunt, disks of weariness hollowed beneath his cheek bones. He looked like a man who had travelled a hundred miles.

"I could see his bones look out," McLeod told us some months later. "I had a vision of his skull, if you know what I mean. He had been chasing the mare through those hills, herding her alone and on foot, for two months. He was run ragged."

Tay John stood some moments in silence, his left arm, now without its sling, held up, the reddened end of the stump showing in the sleeve of his buckskin shirt. He glanced down to it, brandished it. "Funny, eh? Feels funny, too. Always cold. The wind blows in there – right into here." He touched his stomach with the stump.

From his right hand hung long strands of cream-coloured hair, trailing in the breeze rising from down the valley. Following McLeod's eyes he raised his hand. "From her tail," he said. "She left it on the bushes along the trail."

It was his title to the mare, a few wisps of hair from her tail. When he found her he would put them back again where they belonged – as if carried on among mountains and forests, it was the children's blindfold game – with the coming night for blindfold and a horse loose somewhere in the valley for target.

In the morning Tay John, after passing the night at McLeod's cabin, found the mare's tracks and followed them to the ford on the Athabaska river. They were two days old. Yet among the maze of the prints left by other horses, among the moose-tracks and deer-tracks, he picked them out with assurance.

"I don't know how you do it, Tay John," McLeod said.

The other grunted. Tracking was a game he enjoyed.

"She's gone across the river," he said. "She's gone to her home range in the foothills. Grass country there that she knows."

"Yes – and probably she's in heat. When they're in heat, they travel," McLeod agreed.

Nothing would satisfy Tay John but that McLeod would put him across the river. An old dugout canoe was hidden under some willows half a mile above the ford. It served McLeod for his occasional trips back and forth over the water. He gave Tay John a pack sack with flour and bacon, and after they had crossed the river saw him disappear into the timber on the eastern slope of the valley.

Somehow he doubted Tay John would find the mare. It was a big piece of country for one man afoot to cover. A horse, which is only a stomach on four legs, will wander far off the trail in search of feed – or, if taken by impulse to be with his kind, will travel fast and hard along it. Either alternative made Tay John's task a hard one.

For several days McLeod paddled across the river in the afternoons, expecting to find his yellow-haired friend waiting to be taken back to Solomon's Flats – but Tay John did not return until summer had passed and the poplar leaves flamed with frost.

He rode then into the clearing by McLeod's cabin on a black and white pinto, at the head of a string of packhorses, with a cook, a horse wrangler and probably the first pair of tourists to stop on the flats.

It was a transformation to cause the stocky Scots trader to pause and rub his bald head, to purse his lips and whistle.

Tay John's pinto, a gelding, was a medium-sized beast with a pink nose, white-rimmed eyes, and arched neck. He stepped high, putting his small black hoofs so lightly on the ground that beneath them the grass seemed rooted in pliant springs. Tay John, too, wore an entirely new outfit of clothes – dark doeskin trousers, a blue woollen shirt, a white caribou-hide vest, and on his head, for the first time that McLeod was aware of, he had a black high-crowned Stetson. His old buck-skin shirt was tied behind his saddle.

It was, however, the woman on a white horse immediately behind him who took McLeod's eye. She was small, young, not much more than a girl, dressed in black, a split skirt and high-heeled riding boots. She held a crumpled fedora hat in her hand and the late sunlight of the afternoon kindled her fluffy auburn-tinted hair. She had very wide, very blue eyes with long fair lashes, and these, with her lips, full, red and slightly parted, and the small purple bow at her throat gave to her face an expression of sustained surprise at what she saw about her – at McLeod standing in his cabin door, to whom passing close she waved a chubby gloved hand and said, "Hello; nice place you have here." She indicated the mountains, the valley, the poplar-trees.

"Glad you like it," called back McLeod.

She turned in her saddle to show a responsive smile.

When she had gone on, McLeod sniffed the air, for she left behind her a heavy scent of perfume. It seemed to rise from the ground at his feet, above the odours of saddle leather, of sweating horse-hide and sweated blankets. It was so marked he thought of it in terms of colour, the colour of the bow at her throat – a pillar of purple flame. Somehow, too, it reminded him of musk, of the beaver castor men rub upon their traps.

That evening she and her husband called at his cabin, walking over from their camp a mile away upon the flats. During the hour they passed with him McLeod learned their name was Alderson – he a mining engineer from the south of England sent out to investigate coal properties along the pro-jected right of way of the railway. He had heard of one prospect beyond the head of the Solomon, and although it was some-what distant, after meeting Tay John he had decided to go in to see it and later to extend his trip into the sheep-hunting country.

And his wife? Oh, no, she wasn't English. She was a "United Stater" he informed McLeod, with the air of one referring to a distant and almost forgotten species of the human race. It was her first trip into the West and her first experience of any sort with horses.

"What Julia wonders," he said, "is how horses can be so hard to sit on when they're full of grass." He winked a brown, sullen lidded eye at McLeod.

"Did you hear me, Julia?" he said over his shoulder. "We're talking about horses." Julia was in the far part of the room, back towards them, inspecting the furniture, the beaded Indian hangings, touching the logs of the walls.

"Yes, I heard you," she said without turning, "but I'm not listening. I don't have to worry about horses until the morning, thank God!"

"There's a woman for you," Alderson said, slapping his knee. "She's not listening, but she heard me." He laughed slowly, deeply, as though he shuffled slack coal in his chest.

He took a pouch out of the pocket of his jacket and set to plugging the dark bowl of his pipe with tobacco. He had wide, big knuckled hands – hands which had been used. His pipe filled and lit, he pulled at a bushy eyebrow, and his long, flat cheek, browned with the sun, shadowed and glowed by the fire. McLeod judged him to be some twenty years older than his wife, somewhere in his middle forties.

Hob-nailed boots were Alderson's only concession to mountain travel. Otherwise his grey tweeds, his flannel shirt with its knitted tie suggested one who had just come in off the golf course, or who had set out for a casual stroll from his house in the suburbs, seen a light in a window and come in to pass the time of day.

He was a man, however, whose strolling had covered a large part of the earth's surface. He had hunted on three continents, but never before in North America. "This was a capital chance for me to see something of the West," he said, "and of how things are done out here. And with a man like Tay John to show one about, well . . ." He spread his hands, raised his brows. "What better luck could we wish for?"

"I think you're right there," McLeod said. "He's an

A.1 man, a first-rate hunter and trapper. You couldn't have a better one for the job if it's sheep and caribou you're after. Yes, I think he's a thoroughly reliable fellow."

"Good. That's exactly my impression," Alderson said.

"I put him over the Athabaska six weeks ago," McLeod said after a time, "and he went off afoot to look for a saddle-mare he had lost."

"Six weeks! We picked him up only ten days ago," Julia put in. "Where could he have been all that time?" She had come to sit on the arm of her husband's chair, and as she spoke ran her fingers through his long iron-grey hair. He frowned, his eyebrows like two black caterpillars, crawling together.

"It's a big piece of country," McLeod said to Julia. "He might have been anywhere."

"But how would he live?"

"He'd live. He'd find a steak in a moose track. And if he didn't he'd snare rabbits."

"But we didn't see any rabbits," Julia said.

"That's the point about rabbits, Julia," Alderson explained. "You snare them first and see them afterwards. It's really a problem in metaphysics."

"I wonder," he added, irrelevantly, to McLeod, "if this same Tay John has ever said 'thank you' in his life?"

"Not to me. But then there's no reason why he should."

"No reason why he should to me, either, I suppose," Alderson said, "but you see we fished him out of the water, saved him from drowning."

"Tay John in the water and drowning?"

"We rescued him," Julia broke in from behind Alderson's chair. "At least, Arthur" – indicating her husband – "and Charlie did."

"There's the question," Alderson said. "We may think we rescued him, but I fancy Tay John looks at it in a different light."

He settled back, legs crossed, puffing his pipe.

McLeod coughed.

Alderson glanced at him suddenly. "Of course, of course," he said. "I was forgetting – about Tay John. You see, it was like this. We were camped two or three days' journey down the Athabaska from here. On the other side."

Alderson said it had been a night of brilliant moon. He had walked out on a sand spit a quarter of a mile above the camp, and noticed what at first appeared to be a log and some branches floating down the river which was running high and fast. The recent spell of excessively warm weather had brought a lot of melted snow from the mountains. Then by the side of what he had taken to be a log, he saw a movement. He saw a hand lifted. He saw all the fingers, outlined for a moment against the water which with the moon on it shone like a great silver coin. "I would not have been surprised, McLeod," he said, "if out of it a sword had been brandished before my eyes."

But no, it was only a hand. Then he saw a man's head and above it in the stream, a horse's head. The horse was swimming against the current, but could not match its flood of water. Horse and man were being carried swiftly down.

"I understood then," Alderson said, "that the spit of sand on which I stood was their only chance. They would come close to it. But I was helpless. What could I do? A rope? None was nearer than the camp. Then I felt someone beside me. It was Charlie, our cook. Charlie doesn't miss a trick. He had been watching the river, too – and with him he had a rope, a lariat belonging to Ed, the horse wrangler. Ed, after his custom, was asleep following supper. Charlie waded into the water. I went with him to steady him, if I could. We were up to our hips when Charlie cast the rope. Tay John was hanging on to his horse's tail. I didn't know then, of course, who he was, nor yet that he had only one hand. He speared the noose of rope on that useless left arm of his. The noose tightened. The line in our hands bid fair to pull us off our feet. Tay John with his right hand hung to his horse's tail, while we pulled on the rope tightened about his other arm. The horse swam against him. His hold broke. We hauled him ashore. The horse was carried down out of our sight, around a bend. Lost, I suppose, for we found no trace of it down river the next day."

Tay John lay between Alderson and Charlie, stretched out straight, face buried in the sand, as if he were taking suck from the earth. He rolled over, sat up, elbows on his knees. He shook his head, spattering their clothes with water. He rose, stood staring at the polished moonlit river. He glanced at Charlie, at Alderson.

"And that one glance of his," Alderson said to McLeod, "made me feel that I had no right where I was at all. I was an interloper. He – well he was something shaped by the river, by the hills around us to their own ends. He didn't say so much as 'thank you,' or allude then, or later, to what he had gone through, from what, through our intervention, he had escaped. Indeed, swimming his horse across the river might have been a habit of his – for the exercise. He saw our camp-fire through the trees and walked towards it. We followed."

"But what in the name of God was he doing putting his horse across the river there?" McLeod asked.

The other knocked his pipe against the stone of the fire-place. He shook his head. "You know as much about it as I do. Wanted to get back to the mountains, I dare say. Misjudged the ford and his horse's feet were swept from under him. For myself I've never asked him, because I fancy he was a bit put out at being found in such a pickle. He possibly even believes that if we hadn't interfered both he and his horse would have got safely enough to shore."

Among them they set Tay John up in a new outfit of clothes which he put on in place of his buckskin trousers and shirt, stretched and soggy with water. This he accepted as a gift and kept. The big hat McLeod saw him wearing when he rode on to the flats had belonged to Alderson. "I could never get accustomed to the damn thing," Alderson said, "and he seemed to want it because the others, Charlie and Ed, were wearing Stetsons." Earlier in the season Alderson had had an assistant with him. It was his saddle Tay John rode.

He stayed with them, not seeming to have anything else in particular to do. He fairly ate them out of camp, eating as though each meal were his last – or his first after a long star-vation – until sweat stood out on his forehead.

Alderson asked him questions about the country. "That's how the hunting trip idea came up," he said. "Tay John had taken a fancy to that pinto he's riding. We made a bargain. He's to have the pinto and a pack pony as payment for taking us into this piece of country over on the Smokey which he says so far has not been hunted at all."

Julia stood again close by her husband's chair regarding McLeod with blue, unblinking eyes. He felt that her eager breasts from beneath her grey blouse regarded him, too. Her pink fingers patted the bow at her throat. Once more he was conscious of the heavy, musk-like perfume which she exuded. Yet it was at the same time apart from her. It had a form and presence of its own, moving among them, coming between them, like a fourth party in the room.

"Of course," Alderson was saying, "I didn't have to ask him who he was. We had heard of Tay John down the line –

of that yellow head, and of his losing his hand in a fight with a grizzly bear."

"However did he come to do that?" Julia demanded of McLeod, as though it might have been a case of mere forgetfulness.

"I guess it was an accident," McLeod said, stirring uneasily in his chair.

"I wanted to put a bandage on it," Julia told him. "It looked so sore and red. I saw him from our tent the first night he was with us, when all the others had gone to bed. He was sitting by the fire with a blanket over his shoulders. He seemed lonely – you know, as if he were remembering things. Once he held up that arm of his and looked at it. I wanted to go out right then – I even had the bandages with me – but Arthur wouldn't let me."

"Of course not," Alderson said. "I wouldn't let you go. It's all healed up long ago. He would have laughed at you."

When they rose to leave he helped Julia with her mackinaw jacket, bending over to button it about her throat.

"The nights are cold up here. You must take care," he said.

"Arthur, I think I'm old enough to look after myself." Julia shook herself free.

"I'm not so sure. . . ."

Outside the door McLeod saw Alderson press her arm against his side.

Returning indoors McLeod stopped on the threshold. The room where the Aldersons had been was hazy with pipe smoke and smoke from the fireplace. Yet to McLeod it seemed not so much the haze of smoke as the purple haze of a woman's perfume. The very logs of the walls appeared to be tinged with its colour as he knew the chinks between them would be strong with its vapours.

He opened the two windows to let the wind blow through, and in the cool air paced nervously back and forth before the dwindling fire.

Candle in hand, shirt-tail against the bow of his legs, approaching his bed he looked closely at the calendar tacked above it – at the white-skinned girl dipping her foot into the pool of water. With one sweep of his hand he ripped the picture from the wall. He tore it into pieces and fed them to the fireplace.

In the morning he would have a chance to speak to Tay John. He would draw him aside. He would tell him to be careful.

But if Tay John asked him why, or of what he was to be careful, McLeod knew he would have no answer.

EIGHT

I f the success of the trip had depended simply upon
hunting theirs would have been a successful one. For they
found game, or Tay John found it for them – sheep, goat,
caribou, two black wolves, and a bear, picking it out day after
day on slopes which to the others' searching eyes seemed
barren, bereft of life. Alderson remarked that their guide could
hear a sheep's heart beat on the other side of a mountain.

But a trip into the hills depends upon many things. This
one, for instance, took its character from a loose stone on a
hillside on which Alderson, during their last morning of
hunting, slipped, turned his ankle, was forced back to camp,
leaving Julia, who had gone out with him, to continue with
Tay John towards a flock of rams some miles away, discovered
the afternoon before grazing close to the edge of snow. There
was a big head among them, a forty-inch curl they thought,
and he was content to let his wife try to bring it down. More
than that, he was eager she should, for Alderson, a keen hunter,
was also an unselfish one.

Tay John had by this time assumed complete command
of the expedition. The others tried for favour before him,

scanning the hillsides as they rode along, seeking, if only for once, to discern the movement of game before his vision fastened upon it. They were not successful.

He had brought them into the high country where the wind blows among the grass roots, where a man's voice is a small thing, his shout a whisper dying in the storm, and they and their horses only a few diligent morsels of life clinging precariously to mountain walls. There, rivers were unnamed, the mountains unnamed, no blazes were upon the trees nor mark of trail upon the sod. They were the first.

And always the wind blew. At times it seemed it would lift them from the ground, blow them from the face of the earth entirely, lift after them into space the very tracks they had left behind. It would blow the thoughts from their heads, speech from their mouths, sight from their eyes – leave nothing at all but the land of mountains waiting for their names, and small creeks flowing into rivers murmuring the names man had yet to utter.

Tay John fired not a shot nor lifted his hand to help with the work of making and breaking camp. He was the guide. He rode before them and walked before them. The farther they reached into the mountains the farther it seemed he withdrew from them. He became taciturn and moody. At night he took his sleeping robe of marmot hides and slept away from the camp, under a tree or on a mossy mound. It was as though he said, "I must pass the days with you, but the nights at least I will have to myself."

According to the evidence that came out later at the trial – Oh, yes, there was a trial of sorts at McLeod's place on Solomon's Flats. A hearing would perhaps be the better name for it. Yes, they gave Tay John a hearing, and before or during that hearing it came out that the night previous to their last hunt while, after supper they were sitting about the camp fire, Julia, to break a long silence, had asked a general question – a very general question indeed.

It was one of those questions a man is ever ready to try to answer because the answer lies so far beyond his rational and conceivable experience. She sat by her husband. Across from her were Charlie the cook, and Ed the horse wrangler, and off from them a bit, squatting on his heels, his knees just touched by the glow of the camp-fire flames, was Tay John. Facing Julia were the doors of the two tents, idly open, maws waiting to consume them in darkness.

"Suppose," she said, lifting her head of auburn hair, "suppose that for each of us, to-night was his last night but one, and that to-morrow you could do anything you wanted to do, be anywhere you liked, what company you desired, what food, anything yours for the asking – for that one day, your last – what would you do?"

She looked at Charlie – a man in his late twenties, face rusted with whiskers. He had watery eyes and stiff straw-like hair, every strand of which seemed to lead an existence of its own apart from the rest, so that it sprouted above his forehead like a bunch of autumn grass. His nose was putty, each morning appearing to have a different shape as if he had slept upon it. Often, too, a tear-drop hung from it, so that, as a precaution before he spoke, Charlie usually sniffed and rubbed the back of his hand across the lower part of his face.

He repeated this gesture now and regarded Julia with some dismay. "Come on, Charlie," she encouraged him, "you're not going to have to do it. It's only a question after all."

"Gee, Mrs. Alderson, I don't know. I've never thought about a thing like that."

"Now, Charlie . . ."

"Well, perhaps . . . I don't know, but perhaps I'd have a good meal and get drunk afterwards." Charlie, embarrassed by his confession, threw another log on the fire and the flames showed a flush rising on his long, thin neck.

Nevertheless, it was the same Charlie who, during the events of the next few days, kept his head, noticed what was happening about him, took the lead when leadership was necessary.

"That's an idea at any rate, I must admit," Julia commented.

"And what do you think, Ed?" Julia turned to the horse wrangler – an older man, with a tough, short body, a small, round, closely cropped head. He resembled, with his feet crossed under him, nothing more than a squat pine-stump with a fire-blackened stone set upon it – such as one finds sometimes to mark a trail across a *brulé*.

Before Ed replied he stared back at Julia. His hard eyes bored into her. The silence became long and marked. Her face drained of blood.

"Well?" Alderson said suddenly. "Out with it, man! Say your say and be done."

"Arthur!" Julia put a hand upon his knee.

"It's an absurd question to ask anyone," he said to her. He implied it was a particularly absurd question to ask Ed. He muttered something about imagination and fell to filling his pipe.

Ed interrupted. He shook his shoulders. The glaze left his vision. "If I could do anything at all I wanted for one day? . . . Then maybe I'd go to Montreal. I've always sort of wanted to go there. I'd eat in a restaurant, a French one with waitresses, and then . . . well then . . ." His voice stumbled into incoherence. He jabbed a stick of firewood into the ground, outraged at the very earth which bore him.

"Your question is certainly one to arouse the appetites," Alderson remarked to Julia.

"And what would you do with it?" She confronted him with unwonted sharpness.

"My last day? . . . why hope to pass it with you, my dear. But because it seems it isn't my last day and to-morrow Tay John tells us we have some climbing to do after that ram he saw to-day, I'm going to turn in. You'll excuse me." Alderson rose, patted her head as if she were a child at his knee, and went into his tent.

Ed stretched. He said he guessed he'd hit the hay as well.

Tay John, somewhat behind Charlie, had not been asked. He had listened. He wasn't above the question, nor above those involved in it. But something about him was, suggesting a wisdom the others searched for, a knowledge of the Dark Stranger who moved in their words, one whose voice he knew, whose call he had heard, whose gaze he had met.

"What do you think about it, Tay John?" Charlie, who did not wish Tay John to feel he was being wilfully excluded, startled Julia by his question.

Tay John, ignoring Charlie, looked across the fire towards her, seeming not to look at her so much as to include her in a general survey of his surroundings. As his head turned, his long yellow hair brushed the shoulders of his buckskin shirt, and the left forearm, with its empty cuff, hung pendulous from the elbow cocked upon his knee. He flipped a cigarette stub from him.

Then he looked more closely at Julia. He considered. His glance passed on, over her into the tree tops, into the great wide heavens of the northern night.

"I guess, I go hunting," he said.

"You would only do what you are doing now?" Julia was unbelieving.

"Of course . . ."

Tay John rose, left Charlie and Julia by the fire.

"A queer guy," Charlie murmured.

"Queer? I don't know whether it's that," Julia replied. "But he's so strong, so sure – so sure sometimes he makes me afraid."

The next morning they were astir early. During breakfast Tay John pointed to a string of goat, high up, migrating across a rocky mountainside. "A storm is coming," he said. "A big one from the north. Not to-day, but maybe to-morrow or the day after. See – the goats come to this side of the mountain for shelter. They are the ones that know."

As was usual when they were hunting, Charlie put a lunch up for them, and while he and Ed stayed in camp Tay John led Alderson and Julia, each of the last two carrying a rifle, off into the alplands above. He said they would have four or perhaps five miles to walk and climb for a shot at the ram he had picked out for them. Alderson already had a fair sized head to his credit. This one was to be Julia's, and promised to be the best of the trip.

Shortly before noon Alderson returned to camp. He was limping and helped himself along with a dead branch of spruce. He had slipped on a stone, turned his ankle, and unable to keep pace with the others had sent Julia on with Tay John to the flock of sheep they could discern still some miles away and higher up.

They had been well above the timber, and, before drop-ping down to camp, Alderson had looked back to watch the other two crossing a small draw with snow banked at its head. Tay John paused to give Julia his hand. She seemed very small up there, a brown-headed girl searching for something she had lost. Alderson hobbled the three miles into camp.

"Gee, that's tough luck, Mr. Alderson," Charlie consoled him, regarding the injured ankle, and making him tea and a fresh bannock.

"When do you think they'll be back, Charlie?" Alderson asked later, after he had bathed his foot and Charlie had rubbed it for him.

"Oh, they'll be back for supper. Tay John's not the fellow to miss a meal if he can help it."

When Ed came in from looking after the horses, Alderson inquired if he thought the weather was going to break. Ed wasn't sure. "I guess it'll hold for a few days yet," he said.

As the day wore on Alderson became increasingly rest-less. Though it pained him to walk, he limped back and forth across the camping place, like a captain on his bridge, staring up the valley whence Julia and Tay John should appear.

They delayed supper until after dark. They listened for the sound of voices, the crack of a branch – anything to indi-cate that Tay John and Julia were returning. But nothing broke through the wall of darkness. Night was around them, and above them. Clouds hid the stars. Night was a great dark bird shadowing them with its wings, and like down from those wings snow began to fall. It was not white so much as an intensification of the dark, making the obscurity palpable. They were being touched by night itself. The flakes upon their eyelids were the caress of sleep. Somewhere a wolf howled – a being from another planet lost upon the earth.

"My God, Charlie!" Alderson said, "what do you think has happened? They've had time and more to get back to us."

"Don't you worry, Mr. Alderson. They're all right. Perhaps Mrs. Alderson got tired. They're probably sitting around a fire, just like we are, waiting till it's light enough to travel. They've been benighted, that's all. No need to worry with Tay John. He could find his way through tar, if he had to. But he's saving Mrs. Alderson, that's what he's doing."

"Around a fire like we are?" Alderson's long face twitched. "My wife up there alone for the night, with a yellow-haired Indian fellow? Come, Ed, we're going out to find them."

Across the fire he addressed the horse wrangler, who shook his head. "No, not now," Ed said. "We've got to wait till daylight. Why, I couldn't even find the horses – and you can't travel afoot. Besides they'll be in here by then."

"Sure," Charlie said, "they'll be in here by then."

In the dark and the snow they were helpless as three men locked in a room. They might have made a move, but away from their camp they could not have seen their hands before their faces.

Charlie built up a fire. It burned all night. They sat about it, nodding, dozing, awaking with sudden starts. Once Ed jumped up, tossing from his shoulder the blanket he had pulled around him to shed the snow, and ran to the circled edge of firelight, listening to the bells of his horses. "A bear or moose must have frightened them," he muttered. "They're galloping. They'll be miles away in the morning." He put on his boots. "Oh, hell!" he said, taking them off again, "it's only another hour. I might as well wait till I can see."

He was on his way down the trail before the dawn broke like a pale, uneasy trembling of the night. He brought the horses back, caught three of them and tied them up.

"Mr. Alderson – Mr. Alderson!" he shouted while he was still busy at his task. "Something funny's happened. Tay John's horse is gone, that black and white pinto, and the white horse Mrs. Alderson rides and Mike, the bay pack pony."

"Gone? You mean disappeared?" asked Alderson.

"No. Someone's taken them. See, the saddles are gone, too." He pointed to the saddles and rigging piled under canvas some fifty yards away from the tents. "Someone came in there during the night while we were sitting around the fire."

"Someone?" Alderson's eyes wavered. "Who do you mean? Who could do that, while we were around the fire?"

"There's no one in this neck of the woods but Tay John and ourselves. You remember I heard the horses running? Well, that's when he caught them, after he got the saddles and the rest of the rigging from the pile. A natural man couldn't have done it without us hearing. He must have put cotton wool in our ears first."

"You mean he and my wife! . . ." Alderson was on his feet, forgetful of his sore ankle, pacing by the fire.

But Ed had vanished into the bush. He returned. "It was him all right," he announced. "I've just been up to where he left his sleeping bag – that fleabag of his. It's gone, and his rifle too. It's all gone."

"Now, Mr. Alderson," Charlie said, looking up from his frying pan, "take it easy. Perhaps he needed those horses to get her back here. A man never knows."

"Ed, how long till you're ready? We can't sit about like this doing nothing," Alderson exclaimed.

"As soon as you're ready. Soon as I've had a cup of coffee we'll be on our way. We'll light right out after them. We can track those horses in the snow."

Day showed winter camped on the mountain tops and by the camp spruce-trees, mantled with snow, stood like hooded strangers. And from among them, as Alderson and Ed gulped hot coffee, Julia rode into the clearing. Yet she did not ride so much as she appeared by a trick of magic – a white faced woman on a white horse out of the white hung trees. There was that about her to remind them, if only for a moment, of pictures from old books of castles and knights with banners. A suggestion of a wandering and abandoned Lady Godiva. Her cheeks were pinched, but a hectic red was on them. Her blue eyes were wide as if they had just looked upon a revelation. During the night, or during the ride back, her hair had come undone. A plait of it hung down her shoulder and spread its strands across her breast. Her mackinaw jacket and the grey blouse beneath it were ripped, possibly torn on the bushes, and though she tried, pulling tight the rent in her mackinaw, to conceal it, the white skin of her breast showed, as if, do what she would, it would see the world on its own account. For all that, she surveyed the three men for an instant in an attitude of unyielding dignity. It seemed that from her height she would smile on them.

Alderson limped towards her, his lips moving but no word coming from them. Seeing him before her, she started. She tightened the lines on her horse, as if to turn him back again into the timber. It was as though, against her wish, she had been driven into the clearing, to the tent door which she had left not twenty-four hours earlier. She regarded those before her as unreal. Then the mood passed like a shadow from her face, leaving in its place the mark of struggle, a breathlessness. She struggled to breathe. She gasped. The sound of her intaken breath cut across the stillness. Charlie's hand opened and the cup in his fingers dropped to the ground and rolled into the fire. Ed stared, mouth agape. All at once Julia's face contorted, became the face of an old woman in repose. She sobbed.

Alderson pulled her from the saddle. He tried to cover her from sight, arms outstretched, as if in truth she were naked.

She fell against him, head on his shoulder.

Alderson took her to his tent. In a moment he put his head out of the door. His jaw was trembling, his lips slack. It was like the head collared with canvas at a country fair at which the customers shy wooden balls. It wavered. It slacked and strained the tent walls. "Charlie!" he called, "some coffee. Quick! Quick, man! Hurry!"

Later Ed and Charlie sat by the fire, drinking coffee, smoking, listening to the murmur of voices within the tent.

They heard Julia say, "He's a brute, what a brute! He left me for hours – hours, Arthur, all alone, by a fire while he came down here. He said he was going to get Ed and come back with the horses. He came back alone . . . in the dark."

Alderson spoke in a low voice, trying to make her speak more calmly, to confine her voice within the tent.

"What do I care?" she cried. "Let them hear." The notion came to Charlie that she wished them to hear. "Let everyone hear. You're the one who is to blame. You left me alone with him. . . . I tell you we couldn't get back last night. We walked so far. I couldn't walk another step. That's why he came down here to get the horses. No – he's not coming back. He said, when I missed the ram, the hunting was over now, and he's gone and taken the two horses you promised him."

Charlie heard her sobbing and wondered why she cried. Her voice was muffled. The tent wall bulged, the shape of a head showing beneath it. The whole tent shook as though within it they contended together.

Julia's voice rose again. "I tell you, you don't know what I went through. Tay John. . . . Arthur, Arthur, don't you understand? – Are you blind? – he – he – imposed himself upon me."

"*Jesus!*" Ed said, rising to his feet and digging a toe into the ground.

Alderson burst from the tent, hair upended, like a man pursued. "Ed – the horses!"

Ed threw his hat down and jumped on it. "Let me go alone, Mr. Alderson. I'll go out and bring the one-armed bastard in."

Charlie got to his feet, from where he had been sucking a dead cigarette by the fire. He rubbed his hand across his nose. "Say," he said, looking at Ed, "anyone would think to see you this was your affair and not Mr. Alderson's. Now I'm going to tell you something – see? You're not going out after Tay John, and Mr. Alderson's not going after him either." The other two stepped back, astounded that Charlie should attempt to take command. Charlie paused. Then he said to Alderson:

"Mr. Alderson, we've got to keep our heads. Ed and me here couldn't help hearing some of the things you and Mrs. Alderson were talking about in the tent – but Ed hasn't got any more chance of catching Tay John than he has of catching a caribou by its tail. The people to handle this, if you want it handled that way, are the police, the Royal North-West Mounted, they're the fellows, and what we'd better do is pull out now – all of us – and go back to Solomon's Flats to see what we can do down there."

Charlie's opinion, which he revealed later, one perhaps based upon bitter personal experience, was that a man alone, no matter how strong, how wily, how persevering, would find it impossible to "impose himself" – ("And I never heard it put quite that way before," he said) – upon a woman if she were unwilling. "Unless, of course, he choked her first, or beat her into insensibility. Of course he may have tried," Charlie added.

"And there wasn't a mark on her," he said. "I figured she was sore and maybe frightened at being left alone while Tay John went for the horses. Or maybe she just wanted to impress her husband. I don't know nothing about it – but that's the way I figured it out. Maybe," he suggested on a more private occasion, "she wanted it all along – still then why would she talk about it? And why would Tay John pull out the way he did?"

Charlie at the time kept his conjectures to himself, but his advice was taken and they pulled out down the valley, back the way they had come. He led them back. He was an old hand on the trail and hired out as cook not because he was unable to manage horses but because he preferred the easier and better paid job of cooking.

It was a sober, restrained party. A dreary trip, snow, frozen pack ropes, brittle ice in the muskegs that cut the horses below the fetlocks. Julia and Alderson rode silently, rarely speaking even at meals. She seemed suddenly mature. Lines were in the corners of her eyes, webbed. Spiders had been working there. Alderson spoke only to curse his horse, the weather, the country.

Sometimes Julia stopped to look back along the trail. But there was nothing there. *He* wasn't there at any rate, following. All she saw was rushing river water, and the forest sorrowing, and flakes of snow settling from the dusk of the sky. Somewhere out beyond, perhaps on a ridge in the hunting country, was a figure on a pinto horse, long yellow hair blowing in the wind.

Charlie did not expect to find the Mounted Police on Solomon's Flat, but he hoped that by the time they reached there Alderson would have cooled down a bit. He was impressed by the fact that as the days went on it was Alderson, more than Julia, who desired to bring Tay John to what he called "justice." Ed, too, was determined that something, he wasn't quite sure what, should be done. Indeed, it was the men of the party who seemed to be the ones most offended. Julia, if anything, to Charlie's eyes, sat her horse with more assurance than before, and worry, which had left its mark upon her, he suspected had to do less with what had happened than with the shape of events to come.

As luck would have it, they met up with the police at McLeod's cabin. They were staying there a day or two. McLeod was glad to have them with him as his friends on their visits up and down the valley, this, though he was a trader, and perhaps, like the rest of them, some of his transactions wouldn't stand too close a scrutiny. The trader's rum, for instance, for the Indian trappers. He had nothing really to fear, of course. He was honest – except in his trading, which, like all business, is sometimes a licensed form of dishonesty.

There were two Mounties. One of them a young lad, barely past his majority, fresh out from England. He was long and lanky, long fingered, long armed, long faced, long nosed. His tan boot toes stuck far out in front of him. He didn't walk. He merely shifted his feet from place to place and managed to balance above them. He had large ears, cupped forward, to catch all that was going on. They enclosed his face like a set of parentheses. He was eager, red-cheeked, all agog. This was his first long patrol. They were after whisky smugglers beyond the end of Steel.

"I say, this *is* exciting," he said, when he heard what was in the wind. "A half-breed fellow, eh? A trapper? Fancy that!" He was ready to run out of the door then and there and up a mountain-side. Alderson had spoken to his superior, a Canadian by the name of Tatlow, an old-timer who had been through the Riel Rebellion, heavy, thick set, chest bulging under his red tunic, nodding his head slowly while he listened. He tilted a chair back against the counter in McLeod's store, knotted a pair of knob-knuckled hands. His forehead, shielded by his hat from the sun, was deadly white against the tan of his cheeks, his pale eyes under greying brows like a pair of half-opened oysters. They seemed at any moment about to shut tight, to cut off from him for ever the sight of that world with which, his attitude suggested, he was profoundly bored.

"Of course, Mr. Alderson," he said, "this is somewhat irregular, you know. You come to me and ask me to help you, yet your wife, who I take it is the injured party, refuses to see me, much less to swear out a complaint."

Alderson executed two paces towards the door and turned again towards Tatlow, hands beating behind his back. "You must understand, Sergeant. She – well, after her experience, she is hardly herself. What could you expect? But if she were confronted by the man . . . Sergeant, believe me, she won't so much as leave her tent, much less talk to anyone."

Tatlow turned to McLeod.

"Where does this fellow hang out?" he wanted to know in a voice that he might have used to inquire about the fishing in Solomon creek.

"An old cabin up above Rock Lake," McLeod answered.

"Not far?"

"No; a couple of days perhaps."

"Now, Mr. Alderson," said Tatlow, "I'll tell you what I'll do. You say you think this Tay John johnny has left the country. If he has there would be a presumption – we would have to go after him. But if he hasn't . . . well then we'll probably find him at his cabin up above this lake."

Porter, the young fellow with the ears, exclaimed, made some sort of noise or other. He probably wanted to cheer. Here was the chance for him to do the kind of thing he had read about – like a story in *Chums*, chasing a half-breed hunter through the mountains.

Tatlow looked at him, his cold grey eye opening, then clamping shut. Porter, standing against the wall, blushed. He began to roll himself a cigarette. Alderson, too, for an instant seemed about to speak to him to draw his attention to the issues involved.

Tatlow continued: "Mr. Porter, with three of your horses and your man to look after them for him, will go up there to this cabin. If Tay John is there he will request, only request mind you, that he come down here. If he refuses – in that case, I assure you, we will know what to do. For the time being you will let the matter rest with us, it being understood of course that you and your wife will remain here on the flats until Mr. Porter returns."

Porter went out in the morning, his rifle, carrying its dark dream of eternity, conspicuously slung from his saddle. Ed went with him.

In four days they returned, with Tay John on his pinto horse – and with Porter as Tay John's advocate. On the way down Tay John had shown him how to stalk a moose. "The man has eyes," Porter said, "eyes, eyes. That moose – why I would have passed him by. Never seen him. Why this country's alive with game and I've gone through it without seeing a rabbit, not even a mouse."

Porter implied that, as a result of his two days on the trail with Tay John, life for him had taken an entirely new turn. The hidden was now revealed.

It was in the afternoon when Tatlow called Tay John in to see him in McLeod's back room. They had a talk together, then Alderson and Julia were sent for. Tatlow sat by the table before the fireplace, some papers scattered upon it, enough to shield its stain of blood. Tay John faced him from the other side of the room, back against the wall. By his side stood Porter. McLeod was in a corner on a box, face cupped in his hands and staring at the floor.

Alderson came in.

The spring had gone from his step, the easy, friendly confidence from his face. He was like one who himself expected sentence. He held his eyes from the wall where Tay John stood.

"But your wife, Mr. Alderson. Your wife must come in," said Tatlow, raising his head.

"She won't come. She refuses. I've done my best." He lifted his hands, dropped them to his sides, where they hung heavy, helpless, pendulous, as if by ropes from his shoulders.

"Mr. Alderson – we have done our best, too. This man here" – indicating Tay John – "has done his best. He has travelled down hear to clear himself. Will you be good enough to convey my compliments to Mrs. Alderson and inform her that she *must* appear?"

When Alderson came in with Julia, McLeod was shocked by the change that had come over her. Her eyes, those wide blue eyes rimmed with surprise and long lashes, were reddened as if by dust and wind. The lustre seemed to have gone from her hair. Her feet in their small riding boots moved uneasily upon the floor, as if it were hot and she could find no place to stand with ease. She held a mackinaw over her shoulders.

Tatlow said: "Mrs. Alderson, we are very sorry to trouble you, but I think you are acquainted with the circumstances which have prompted us to do so."

Julia bit her lip.

"This man" – Tatlow nodded towards Tay John – "I believe you know him?"

Julia said "Yes." It was a whisper.

"Will you tell me, then, what you know about him."

"He was our guide."

Tatlow waited.

"Is that all you have to say?"

"He was our guide. We went hunting with him."

"Mrs. Alderson . . . perhaps if you would look at Tay John it would refresh your memory."

Tay John straightened against the wall. McLeod, watching his strong brown neck where it broadened beneath the open collar of his buckskin shirt into his shoulders, saw the bulge of a great artery. He saw the pulse beat, but so slowly that in the stillness he set to counting it. It was no more than fifty to the minute.

Under that yellow head he wondered what thoughts were beating with it – prison, escape, remorse? Who knows, after all, what transpires behind another's forehead? What broodings, what echoes linger, what golden visions, what cries, what sighs, what sorrows, what hopes, what regrets live on and grow, entwine and merge and for ever battle in another's mind – the mind, the dark vessel, the urn of blood and shadow, the place of silence behind our eyes, borne by each of us upon his shoulders like a penance for his days above the ground?

Julia seemed unable to lift her eyes from the floor at Tay John's feet.

"But," insisted Tatlow, taking things into his own hands and putting a leading question, "isn't this the man you said who . . ." He spread his hands, picked up a pencil and commenced to play idly with it among the papers on the table top.

Julia had a small white handkerchief. She deliberately tore it into shreds, letting them fall, one by one, to the floor.

"Julia!" Alderson's voice, coming from the shadows where he sat, carried entreaty, reproach, dismay.

"Mr. Alderson, if you please!" Tatlow turned on him.

"Then, Mrs. Alderson," he said, "since you can tell us nothing, perhaps Tay John can. Tay John, step out here and tell us what you have already told me."

Tay John obeyed. He stepped forward. He braced his feet wide, as if he felt the roll of the earth beneath them. Though shorter than Porter by half a head he seemed the tallest man in the room.

"Well, Tay John?" Tatlow said.

Tay John stared back at him, but did not speak.

"Tay John – did you tell me the truth earlier this afternoon?"

"I do not lie," Tay John said.

"Very well. You may step back again."

Tatlow turned to Julia. "You have heard, Mrs. Alderson, what Tay John has said. That he has told me the truth. According to that he did the thing which, under the circumstances, he was justified in doing. He brought your horse to you, when you could not walk to camp. Unless you tell me something different, I have no recourse but to believe him. While he was away he left you by a camp-fire against a rock. Perhaps you were unduly frightened? Might that be so?"

Julia hung her head.

"Mrs. Alderson, you must know you are making things most difficult."

Julia faced him in sudden defiance. She looked about the room, at Tay John first, at Porter, at McLeod, at her husband and finally back at Tatlow himself. Her eyes lightened and her cheeks mottled with colour.

"I have nothing to change nor to add," she said. "Tay John was a good man and did everything for us he could on all occasions. Is that all, Mr. Tatlow?"

"That is all."

Julia turned and ran out of the door. She was out of it, through the next room, into her tent, before the others had pulled themselves together.

In the outer room, where with Charlie he had been standing, Ed, when he heard what had happened, banged his fist into his palm. "Damn me!" he said.

"Keep your mouth shut," said Charlie, "and mind your own business."

Alderson went up to Tay John.

"Tay John," he said, "I am sorry. I did not know." He held out his hand.

Tay John, pushing him aside, walked out.

McLeod hurried after him. He wished to assure him that he had had nothing to do with what had happened. They had used his cabin. He could not help it. But Tay John was in the saddle.

The wind, studded with snow, was blowing from the north. The pinto horse, waiting, tied to a poplar, was cold. Mounted, he bucked, and Tay John, left arm lifted high for balance, saw his black Stetson hat, jarred from his head, fall to the ground. When his horse had quietened, he picked up the halter shank of his pack pony, and looped it about his saddle horn. McLeod shouted. Tay John did not turn. He jogged off across the clearing, merging with the curtain of snow, becoming less a man than a movement. He did not leave so much as he disappeared from view, his proportions whittled by mist and distance. He left his hat discarded where it had fallen. He renounced it entirely.

The wind lifted the hat and bowled it across the flats. Ed was on his way out to look for the horses, Alderson having given him orders to make things ready for an immediate departure.

"But it'll be dark before I even get the horses in," Ed protested.

"I don't care if it's Thursday midnight," Alderson said. "You get your horses in and we leave at once."

Now Ed saw the hat running before him.

"Waugh! There's his hat!" he shouted as though all day long he had been looking for it. He let out a further shout and took after it. Charlie, going to the cook tent to cook supper before they pulled out, looked over his shoulder, and ran with him. Porter, the lanky Mountie, was standing in the doorway of the cabin with McLeod. He pricked up his ears like a hound at the sound of the horn, and without a word, but with a glance at McLeod offering apology, joined in the chase. They reached the hat together, fell upon it, tussled, pulled, struggled, rolled into a hollow above whose edges Ed's riding boots showed for a moment.

Porter emerged first, running, the hat under his arm. Charlie and Ed pursued him, hallooing.

Panting, Porter handed the crumpled hat to McLeod. "Keep it for him," he said.

Tatlow came out of the door. He observed Porter's dishevelled tunic. "Hm! . . . youthful exuberance," he said. "Wasted effort. . . . I suppose you think he's going to come back for it?" nodding at the hat held by McLeod.

Squinting his eyes at Alderson who walked restlessly before his tent, Tatlow pulled on his gloves.

"Well," he said, "my guess is that this time he won't."

PART THREE

EVIDENCE — WITHOUT A FINDING

NINE

Tay John had met the new – the world of authority and discipline moving with the railway into the mountains. Yet, perhaps it was not quite new. Perhaps it was only the memory of an earlier authority and discipline – that of the people among whom he was born, who lived beyond the mountains, from whose ways and exactions the discordant heritage of his yellow hair had prompted him to flee.

He had fled from the old. He looked for the new. Yet there is nothing new – these words, nor their meaning – nothing really new in the sense of arrival in the world unless an odd meteor here and there. We have half a million tons of them and their dust a year. To-day was implicit in time's beginning. All that is, was. Somewhere light glowed in the first vast and awful darkness, and darkness is the hub of light. Imprisoned in its fires which brighten and make visible the universe, and shine upon man's face, is the core, the centre, the hard unity of the sun, and it is dark.

All that is not seen is dark. Light lives only in man's vision. Past our stars, we think, is darkness. But here, we say, is light. Here is light where once was darkness, and beyond it, farther than our eyes can see, than our greatest telescope can pierce, is darkness still.

Men walk upon the earth in light, trailing their shadows that are the day's memories of the night. For each man his shadow is his dark garment, formed to the image of his end, sombre and obscure as his own beginning. It is his shroud, awaiting him by his mother's womb lest he forget what, with his first breath of life, he no longer remembers. Sometimes when we are older there is a glimpse. It appears we are returning. We have made the circle.

Our life, our brief eternity, our to-day is but the twilight between our yesterday and our to-morrow. To-day we would escape from both – for ever. It is the promise our hope denies us – because our hope is immeasurable as the vanity that prompts it. Man, if he could, so vain he is, would lift his shadow from the ground and with his blunted fingers shape it. Yet he cannot – for the substance of the shadow is in the fingers that would turn it, and its form, that makes it whole, lies tight upon the earth from which they would remove it.

Then we cry, we of the West, we Westerners, we who have come here to sit below the mountains – for your Westerner is not only the man born here, blind, unknowing, dropped by his mother upon the ground, but also one who came with his eyes open, passing other lands upon the way – Give us new earth, we cry; new places, that we may see our shadows shaped in forms that man has never seen before. Let us travel on so quickly, let us go so far that our shadows, like ourselves, grow lean with our journeys. Let to-morrow become yesterday, now, this instant, while we speak. Let us go on so quickly that we see the future as the past. Let us look into the new land, beyond the wall that fronts our eyes, over the pass, beyond the source of the river. Let us look into the country beyond the mountains.

Illusions? Fantasy? Remember that I speak to you in the country of illusion, where a chain of mountains in the distance seems no more than a dog might leap across, or where on a clear winter's day a mountain thirty miles away seems so close that you might stretch out your hand and lean against it. Remember the cold silence that is a hum in your ears, and the river murmur that is a sort of silence.

But illusion may be more than that; it may become the power to believe, to hope, the callous incapacity to doubt. I think of my friend Alf Dobble, unwitting contriver and prompter for Tay John. Illusions were more real to him than the dark pine-trees which gave logs for his buildings. For he called himself a builder. "Building for the future" was his phrase.

And of the present and its promise, and of himself within it, he had no more idea than a baby newly born. Less perhaps – for a baby tries its strength and tests the strength of that which confines it. But Dobble believed in that for which he hoped. He was a believer.

He believed above all in opportunity. Many men do, but he believed feverishly. His body was heated with his belief. He believed in himself as an instrument – that even out by that lake in the mountains he was the instrument of opportunity, that he served a need. That no one was aware of that need but himself made no difference. To me it seemed no man was ever less needed in the place where he found himself. "Dobble's Future," we called the work he was doing. He had another name for it, for he must be given credit for the courage of his illusions. He could not have been deaf to the fact that many times he was laughed at, openly. He was laughed at the first time I met him. Still his name, the name he gave the place, has lived. It is the name now of a station out there on the railway, a small red station beneath some tall fir-trees, that is all. Still it is a name, and our name, the name we gave to it – well, that's forgotten. It may be that there was more to Dobble than a man would think. I sometimes thought he might have had a quiet life opening oysters behind a bar – in a long white apron, of course. He was such a sanguine fellow.

The railhead by this time had been hammered through the mountains, past Solomon's Flats, across Yellowhead Pass, along the north shore of Yellowhead Lake, and down into the dim canyon country of the Fraser. It was early in 1911.

Alf Dobble had been there before it – by Yellowhead Lake, I mean. He went in there with pack-horses to spy out the land, pick his sites. Yellowhead is a narrow, green lake, its shores wooded with pine- and fir-trees. The Seven Sisters rise sheer above it on the north, an immense wall of rock, green slides below them where grizzlies play, and deep worn trails where mountain goat follow the weather. To the south one sees the summit of Mount Fitzwilliam, a hoary old pyramid of blue and red rock with snow upon its crest. It is set some distance back from the lake, waves of pine ridges breaking against it, to be humbled at its foot. Below these ridges by Yellowhead Lake itself I have sat, since the railway has been laid, and listened to locomotives go by in the night, fire in their bellies, howling far down the valley as though they had lost their way in the mountains. When they passed there would be again in the stillness the sound of lapping water, of wind in the trees, and somewhere out on the lake a splash where a beaver's tail had smacked, or the gurgling deeper note where a fish had jumped. Sometimes there would be a shout from Alf Dobble's place, or a man's laugh, or the hoot of the great horned owl floating above the forest roof. In the winter ice forms three to five feet thick on the lake. It is clean and clear, green as the water, and walking across it before the snow has come, or when the wind has swept it clean of snow, schools of trout dart out from beneath your steps, tickling your toes with their tails.

Alf Dobble never saw the place in the winter. It was summer on his first visit and summer when he went back with his men, as he thought, to stay. But he was gone before the winter. Winter there would have disturbed his illusions. Perhaps he thought of that. I don't know. I think not. It was just his luck. Call it what you will. Across the narrows of the lake from where the railway runs now, below those pine ridges I speak of, there is a flat. Dry ground. A good place for camping. Horse feed. This was the location that Dobble seized upon for what he liked to call "my development."

I met Alf Dobble here in Edmonton, in this very bar. Of course I am telling the story of Tay John, but to that story Dobble had his contribution to make, his word to add. Not that I feel any responsibility to Tay John, nor to his story. No, not at all. His story, such as it is, like himself, would have existed in-dependently of me. Every story – the rough-edged chronicle of a personal destiny – having its source in a past we cannot see, and its reverberations in a future still unlived – man, the child of darkness, walking for a few short moments in unaccustomed light – every story only waits, like a mountain in an untravelled land, for someone to come close, to gaze upon its contours, lay a name upon it, and relate it to the known world. Indeed, to tell a story is to leave most of it untold. You mine it, as you take ore from the mountain. You carry the compass around it. You dig down – and when you have finished, the story remains, some-thing beyond your touch, resistant to your siege; unfathomable, like the heart of the mountain. You have the feeling that you have not reached the story itself, but have merely assaulted the surrounding solitude.

I was not so rash, naturally, as to try to explain this to Alf Dobble. Alf Dobble was not the man for explanations. Besides, at the time I met him, I dare say be had never heard the name of Tay John. The name would have been strange to him. Dobble didn't live to-day. No. He lived in to-morrow. And Tay John – well, to-morrow was a word he had heard upon men's lips. But to-day, to-day, that was the very front of time and he must assail it.

It was in the afternoon, in the early spring, that I met Alf Dobble in the bar here. He picked me out from among the crowd sucking at their glasses. Drink, drink . . . why, to look in on a bar . . . we are the only creatures who drink to increase our thirst.

Dobble said he knew me. More, he knew about me. He had heard things. As he spoke, regarding me with those eyes, coppery sparks glinting in them, their whites turned yellow and bilious, he cocked his head on one side in a way to imply that he had really gone to some trouble about it, suggesting I should at once be alarmed at the extent of his personal knowledge and flattered at the effort he had made to secure it.

"Mr. Denham," he said, "Mr. Denham, we have not met, but I am sure I make no mistake. I know of you. I have heard about you. In fact I . . ." He stopped there, lost for a moment for a word, his mouth held open as if he fought for air. His teeth were rather large, long I should say, rather browned with tobacco, and in the dead centre of the upper row was an immense gold cap. Like his teeth, he was a long man, dressed in a black suit with a long black coat, a flowing bow-tie, and a wide-brimmed flat black hat. He had a high narrow brow, hollows in his cheeks, and a brown moustache touched with grey whose ends drooped as low as his chin. Somewhat the picture of a villain – but not quite. His voice was a bit too loud. He insisted upon being heard not alone by the man he was addressing but by everyone else around. He had a personality. He filled a room. I would have noticed him even if he hadn't approached me.

I insisted upon buying my own drink . . . one shouldn't become indebted to strangers.

"Mr. Denham," he said, after we had smacked our lips a few times over the whisky, "I believe you are familiar with Yellowhead Lake. You know Yellowhead Lake?"

"Passed by there several times with horses," I said.

"Well, the railroad's gone by there now, you know."

I nodded.

"Yes, the railroad." Those words came to me from some-where behind Dobble. It was an echo. I was startled – until I saw their fount. He was a small man. His chin didn't come far above the level of the bar. His clothes looked as though he had slept in them – or as though he had crawled into them from below and his body wriggled in the endeavour to fit them to him. Or he might have been about to emerge entirely from them. A fairish sort of a fellow. Broad faced, red cheeked, and blue eyes that watered. At any moment he might have burst out crying, and I would not have been surprised. He would have cried from pleasure, of course, at being able to corrobo-rate one of Dobble's statements. Yes, he grinned constantly. He was Dobble's factotum, handy man, an uninspired punc-tuation to his master's remarks.

Beyond that one effort he didn't speak again. Dobble paid him no attention. But I knew he was there in the same way that I knew Dobble had buttons for his braces on the back of his trousers. You know . . . something a man would notice the lack of. Without him or someone like him Dobble would not have been Dobble.

"Yes, the railroad, Yellowhead Lake," Dobble went on. "A great country. A place of the future – do you realise that, Mr. Denham?" He swung upon me so suddenly, the ends of his loose bow-tie flapping, his eyes burning, that I stepped back a pace, glass in my hand. He moved between me and the bar. His long forefinger tapped my chest.

"I suppose so," I said. Who was I to challenge his words? There were others there, all listening by now, jarred by the impact of Dobble's staccato utterance.

"Mr. Denham, I come from Colorado. I know mountains when I see them. Now around Yellowhead you have *mountains* . . ." I tried to get back to the bar. I needed its support. I wanted the bartender to smile at me. I felt very much alone affronted by this man from Colorado. After all I had only stopped for a drink. I looked around. One of you might have been there, you know, to give me a hand. But no . . . I had to go through this on my own.

Dobble lowered his voice. He became confidential. "I have a proposition to make to you, Mr. Denham. You may think it queer, coming so sudden as this, but I am a man who knows other men – and who knows himself." He paused, his hand uplifted in the attitude of a preacher. His eyes roved the room. Then: "I know what I want, Mr. Denham. I have studied the human race. You are a man of bearing, integrity, experience. Mr. Denham" – his use of my name was a thrust in the ribs – "I want you to go out there and take charge."

"Of Yellowhead Lake?" I gasped.

"Exactly. . . ." Dobble turned to his glass, lifted it delicately to his lips, brushed a fleck of dust from his coat collar. The matter was settled. Yet after all, I was no god of waters.

Yellowhead Lake, all the tributaries of the Fraser river, had gone on all right up till then without my intervention. They flowed on with their own awful logic to the sea. Besides, I had other things to do.

I said, "Mr. . . . Mr. . . ."

"Dobble – Dobble," he said, "two *b*'s in it."

"Mr. Dobble, I am looking for nothing to do. In the second place; I don't know what you're talking about." I was about to leave. The whole thing was preposterous.

He turned on me. Light from above was reflected on the end of his long, sharp nose. He came closer. His breath was on my face. I felt his body's heat. "Mr. Denham" – it sounded like "missed her" Denham – "you don't understand. This place we speak of, this Yellowhead Lake – it is all to be changed. Changed, changed, do you hear?" He yanked at his moustache. "Yellowhead – the very name will be forgotten in a year, two years. The whole region will be known as the Switzerland of America. There will be a station on the railroad. It will be called Lucerne. Mr. Denham, I am building a *châlet*, yes, a *châlet* on what you now call Yellowhead Lake. For tourists – people will come from all over the world, from all over the world, now that the railroad is built. Opportunity, that's what it is. Don't misunderstand me, please. I do not suggest that you go out there now. No. I am leaving shortly, in a few days, to commence my development work, put the buildings up, you know. The dirty work I will do myself. The logs are cut. But next year, next year, Mr. Denham, I will want a manager there, a man, like yourself, with a bearing, who can meet the world – that is the opportunity I am offering you."

"Meeting the world," I said, "that's Saint Peter's job. And he meets them only one at a time when they're pretty well tired out from the climb." God knows, Dobble was offering me opportunity in capital letters. The world at my threshold and the command of waters at my finger-tips.

"Mr. Denham, you joke. You are not convinced. Tell me, you have been in Switzerland?"

"When I was young – to ski."

"To ski? There's ski-ing there, miles of it above Yellowhead. And tell me this" – he advanced upon me again, his forefinger thumping my vest, that gold tooth shining. I retreated once more from the bar – "Tell me, are there any moose in Switzerland?"

Reluctantly I admitted there were none.

"No; but there are moose at Yellowhead. Hundreds of 'em. Bears, too, and beaver, and mountain goat. . . ."

"And a fool," I muttered, but he didn't hear me.

"People will come there for that," Dobble continued. "Moose grazing by their doors." – I laughed at that – a moose grazing! – "And the *châlet* . . . it will have no equal anywhere – anywhere, Mr. Denham."

By this time he had me back against the wall. At the bar I saw his factotum, whom he called James, grinning. He virtually swallowed his face, that fellow, when he grinned. Some day I was sure he would succeed and die in convulsions. I remember him as a grin that walked – and my torment was for his pleasure. The bartender had a glass held high, polishing it. Seven or eight men were standing in a half-circle about me and Dobble. The man was crazy, and I was involved in his folly. He was dangerous, I realised, as all men of visions are dangerous to a settled way of life and to the tranquillity of our emotions. I determined to leave that vicinity of peril with honour and with dispatch.

"Mr. Dobble," I said, "you have talked to me at some length. Your plan may be a good one – I don't know. Now, see what I have to say. Watch that finger of yours." His finger was still upon my chest. He looked at it then, startled, as if I might have taken it from him. He snatched it back.

I took a deep breath. My chest, you know – I have always been a bit proud of it. Helped me up a lot of hills. I took a deep breath. I spread out my chest and the buttons from my vest flew off. One hit Dobble in the face. They bounced upon the floor. They made a merry tune. Dobble danced back as though he had been stung by hornets. A laugh went up. I left the buttons on the floor and went out to a tailor's to get new ones sewn on. I had turned the tables. The laugh was on him – but it signified nothing. The man was unperturbed.

As I was leaving, he shouted after me, "We will meet again, Mr. Denham." I feared we would, for that summer I had a job packing for a survey party which would take me by Yellowhead Lake with the horses. We used to camp there to give them a rest and feed on the goose grass they like so well. Crossing Yellowhead at the narrows, where it was shallow, we held them across the water from the railway and the trail a day or two till their bellies were rounded out. Yes, Dobble and I would meet again.

TEN

We met in June by Yellowhead. I had nineteen head of horses with me and a second packer to give me a hand with them. We picked the horses up at Fitzhugh – they call the place Jasper now – on the Athabaska, and trailed them up the Miette and over Yellowhead Pass. Our supplies and tents were to be put off the train at Yellowhead Lake and there we were to await the surveyors. They were to be taken up on to the headwaters of the Fraser, sixty miles or more to the south. I would be trailing back and forth all through the summer between the source of that mighty and tempestuous river and the railway, packing food and what-not.

As we came down off the tote road to cross the railway to the narrows of the lake I saw at once that Dobble had not permitted his presence to pass unnoticed. A large sign was by the track. In crudely painted black letters it read: "Lucerne – in the Heart of the Canadian Rockies," a statement so far from literal truth that it was beyond all dispute. Under those words, spelled out in red, I read, "Alf Dobble," then in brackets, in smaller letters, "formerly of Colorado," and below that again, "Proprietor."

"I know," he said when I saw him; "there are no tourists along the line yet. But people will see it – Lucerne – remind them of Switzerland – and they will talk. Talk, Mr. Denham, that's what sells a place. The human tongue is a mighty instrument. I am building the future."

But there was another, more concrete improvement that we, later, were glad of. At first the horses balked, until they accustomed themselves to it – he had built a bridge across the narrows to make easier the freighting of his supplies over the half-mile from the railway to the site where he was erecting his *châlet*. As our horses' hoofs left the bridge we heard the carpenters at their work.

It is difficult to describe what he had there. It was not a town. It more resembled a street in the wilderness. Tall lodge-pole pines crowded close to the long clearing in the forest. As I rode into it at the head of my horses I was confronted by a low, shingle-roofed log structure raised up on the slope that was the southern boundary of the valley. On either side of me, as I approached, were small cabins variously nearing completion, more or less self-contained units where the tourists would live, going up to the main building for meals. Off to the side I saw smoke rising from the bunkhouse, and heard the clatter of pans from the eating-house close by. I was impressed. So much accomplished in so little time. He knew the value of morale among his working staff, he was no stranger to the responsibility of having men working for him, for he had first put up the bunkhouse, the kitchen, and a place to eat. There were perhaps forty men there – Swedes for the axe-work; French-Canadians, carpenters from Edmonton, ordinary working chaps for the other jobs. And the food was good. Indeed, the railway contractors down the line complained that Dobble took their best men by the pay he offered and the working conditions he provided.

It was late afternoon. Dobble was pacing back and forth along this street of his vision, head thrown back – he wore no hat, and his thick half-silvered hair was combed behind his ears. He walked proudly and, of all things, carried a walking stick, swung with rare assurance along that rocky road. The toes of his sharply pointed patent leather shoes glistened. I had looked to see him on some ridgepole giving orders to his men – but no, he was on the ground, his head in the clouds, perhaps, singing with the sound of other men's activity it had engendered. I don't suppose, come to think of it, that with his soft pliant hands he had performed an hour's physical labour in his life. He didn't see me at first. He was staring up at the Seven Sisters, regarding them with a half-quizzical look, as though they too might come within his plans of revision. Yes, that man, if he could, would have reshaped the mountains, too. It must have jarred him a bit to consider that while God had made the world in seven days Alf Dobble would require a summer and part of a winter to build the one he had set his heart upon – his small new world in the mountains.

"Hi!" I shouted.

When he saw me he stopped dead in his tracks. Then he fairly ran up to me, the tails of his long black coat flapping, his tie flapping, his hair bouncing on his head, his arms swinging stiffly from the shoulders. "My Lord," I thought, "the man in his hurry will come apart before he reaches me." He reached me intact.

"Mister Denham! I am delighted! *Dee*-lighted! This is a pleasure, a privilege . . ."

When he retrieved his breath, he said, "My place, my place, don't you want to see it?"

"Yes, of course, but later, please. Meanwhile, Mr. Dobble, you may accept my congratulations. I didn't realise one man could do so much."

That was the truth and he swelled with it. All through our acquaintance he referred to me as "Mister," and I called him "Mr. Dobble." Such small formalities pleased him – for they tended to hold the world at a distance.

He turned from me after I had spoken. "James, James!" he called. James appeared from among the trees. He had been shadowing his master, waiting for his call. He wore a blue mackinaw, baggy trousers, and a pair of immense hob-nailed boots. His clothes were a refuge for his meagre flesh, a place of concealment from his fellow man – always failing him, for they exposed the blue-eyed anguished face like a sweating jack-in-the-box to any who might be passing. That face was spasmed in a grin. It was the same grin – he had been grinning ever since I last had seen him in Edmonton.

"James," Dobble shouted, although the other was close enough by then to touch with his hand, "run, tell the cook . . . Mr. Denham . . ."

"A bit deaf," Dobble explained as James shoved off, barely moving. He approached Dobble on the run, and turned from him with reluctance.

Well, we loosed our horses and went over to the cook-house for a bite to eat before supper. "No need to make camp," Dobble assured me, "I can put you up . . . indefinitely."

Later, when my second packer had left us and we were alone over the teacups, I asked him how things were going.

"You see, Mr. Denham, what I have done. A lot, eh? A lot for the time . . . We have worked hard. My men . . . none better. Hand-picked, Mr. Denham, every one of them. But there are some things . . ."

I waited. I knew it would come out. He offered me a tailor-made cigarette, his initials upon it. I wondered then, as I have since, where he got his money. Someone said mines in Colorado. Someone else an uncle who died in Pretoria. Wherever it came from, it was not the money which interested Dobble. It was the chance money gave him to redeem himself from anonymity. That was his pursuing ghost – he strove that other men might know his name, might see it before them, as on the sign set up by the railway track.

The railway, it appeared, was not affording him the encouragement he had expected. They failed to see the promise of the region. "Look at the Canadian Pacific," he exclaimed, walking up and down before me in that great log-walled room, tall, gaunt, gesturing now and then, his slim, sensuous fingers spread, pausing to inspect a broken finger-nail while he talked – "Banff, Lake Louise – already known half around the world – but these people here actually try to hamper me. Hamper me, Mr. Denham. Of course, I should have looked for that, I suppose. A year from now, next summer, it will be different. My work then will be completed – which is to say, it will be ready to start. That is where you come in. As I told you I feel there is something here for you, enough for both of us. I would not be above considering offering you an interest . . . but now, these days, I am up against a fight. Small things that should never be."

The freight for Dobble's enterprise was dropped by the railway at the sign-post across the narrows of the lake. There was no siding there, of course, which meant that the trains had to stop on the main line. As the spot was on a curve, the super-intendent had suggested that the point of unloading be moved a mile down the track, where the line ran straight and there would not be the same danger of a collision with another train.

"But what will that mean for me, Mr. Denham? It will mean that I will have to construct a mile of road through the timber over soft ground. I have already built the bridge at my own expense. But no, that is not enough. I must be put to more trouble. I tell you, I think these railway officials have their brains in their bowels. They are always thinking of moving. But what can I do? I must build the road. I cannot abandon my work."

He flung himself around. That gold tooth caught the sun's reflection through the window, and gleamed from under his moustache in the dead centre of his pale face. "Do you know," he whispered, so that the cook in the next room might not overhear, "do you know, I believe that that is what some of them would like me to do – to give it up, to lose the money, the time I have invested here. They are as base as that . . . they are afraid I may become a power."

I endeavoured to reassure him. After all, one could not expect too much of railway officials – those rotund figures of immobility presiding over an empire of movement.

"They have their jobs to do, their schemes to spin," I explained.

As I sat there smoking and as Dobble talked, his cigarette gone dead between his finger-tips, work outside ceased. Teamsters walked their horses back to the canvas-topped stables. The clang of the blacksmith's anvil stilled. Hammers and axes were put away. Men's voices, raised in a song of jubilation at the end of the day, drifted in through the open door. The shadow of a pine-tree fell across the window. I heard the note of a robin, and, far back in the forest, the startled chattering of a squirrel. Soon the waiter hammered on the gong and men came in and took their places at the long, board-topped tables, big-booted fellows in overalls and mackinaw shirts, like gods tired with creating, their faces wide and exultant with hard labour achieved. Dobble introduced me to his foreman, Sandy McTavish, small and wiry, with curly upstanding hair and a hand like a knotted piece of wood. He pointed some of the others out to me as they ate, quickly, grimly, without speech that the cook and waiters might finish with their work. A sign read, "No talking during the meal." There was the beetle-browed blacksmith, a man named Pete Murphy from the prairies, and Olaf Johansen, the big Swede, who, with a crew had been on the place all winter skidding the logs down from the hillsides, and others – Mike and Joe, Pete and Jack, Frank and Oscar, Rusty and Shorty, Slim and Hank, names that could be remembered by the timekeeper though the man himself was forgotten.

After supper, down by the lake, I saw a solitary figure in black outlined against the shining waters.

I said to Dobble, "Isn't that a man in a cassock down there by the lake?"

"Yes, a priest," he said, "young Father Rorty. He's been down to the railhead to hold services among the men. He's asked me if he might come back here at times to rest. I put him up in the cabin we have finished. He finds it restful here – you see, I picked the right spot. Restful. He likes the place. Already Lucerne is becoming known."

Later I met the priest – a young, slight man whose voice, while I knew him, was never more than a whispered hoarseness. He used to come very close to me. I would bend down a little that I might hear, for every word was uttered as a confidence. I wondered how he made himself heard to a congregation. A forelock of black hair fell down over his pale high forehead. A small hand, blue veins showing through the smooth skin upon its back, with a thumb slim and straight and almost as long as a finger, would lift to brush it aside. It was a gesture to me symbolic – as if he strove to clear an image from before his fine, blue eyes better to see the world. Yet that lock of black hair returned where it had fallen, and after a while his fingers, forsaking their primary task, would pull it, caress it, smooth it down into the deep crease between his brows. He had yellow, almost brown half-circles under his eyes. When he talked sweat beaded his long upper lip. He seemed a tired man, one who carried his faith as a burden.

For faith may be a heavy burden. There it is distinct from belief. Dobble was a man who believed. What a man believes in, he pleasures in, and his mind assents to his pleasure. A man believes in a thing, as Dobble believed in Lucerne, but a man has faith in a principle, in a doctrine, in a rule of conduct. He trusts to his faith. He may not believe in it. He may even doubt – but a man cannot believe and doubt at one and the same time. When we doubt we begin to learn. Such is the peril of the Roman Catholic priest. He may doubt, yet he must not put his trust in doubt. Warring upon the intangible forces of human destiny, he holds up before men that which they can see, and therefore cannot doubt – the Cross, the Holy Water, the picture of the Virgin Mary. He talks to them of what they can feel. The writings of the Catholic Church are lurid with the flames of Hell. Man can imagine ultimate suffering, for suffering is his lot. But felicity and Heaven – those are dreams. These churchmen, the greatest realists of all time, recognising this, make the fumes of Hell the incense of their Holy Church – the incense through which the priest sees darkly the outer life his cassock forbids him to enter. His followers can suffer and they can dream. Seeing life darkly, he steps carefully, carrying his faith, as I say, like a burden. There is the task of the black-robed men, skirts kicking at their heels – these self-appointed caretakers of eternity. Hell will have its priests intoning masses, promising another heaven, dooming us, by that promise, to further hells.

All of this may seem far away from Father Rorty, the young priest with the blue eyes and the long lashes, beside that mountain lake. Still, I don't know. You must judge of that for yourselves. You have seen priests, too. And this Father Rorty, for all his black robes and his dreams of hell and seas of fire, had an earthly quest as well. There was a brother.

"You have been out here a long time," he confided to me, pulling that long forelock with his nervous thumb and finger, "and you might know. You see, I had a brother. He was twenty years my senior, but I remember him well."

This brother, Father Rorty told me, had been called Red Rorty, and had come out to the mountains in the late 'seventies. He was a big man, tall, fair-haired, and around their home in Ontario was known as the strongest man for miles about. "He would hold me out at arm's length," Father Rorty said. "I was a young lad then of five or six – and sometimes toss me high over his head into the hay loft. He would come up after me and toss me down to another of my brothers waiting below. I was frightened and I suppose I cried, for I recall him laughing at my fear. Still, I was proud to have him as my brother."

This Red Rorty had come out into the Athabaska valley, before the railway, of course. He wrote home from there once or twice. Then they had heard no more from him nor about him. Because of that, from the time Father Rorty entered the Church, he had hoped he might be sent west. Finally he had asked. He saw himself following his brother's footsteps, perhaps coming upon him suddenly in some frontier town or camp.

"For," he said, "it is hard to believe he is dead, a man like that. Sometimes at night, down here by the lake, I listen to the water. I think I hear men's voices coming to me from across it, and among those voices is the voice of my brother Red. He is a big man. You would notice him – of course, now he would be older. I forget that, too. I always see him as he was down there on the farm, laughing, shouting, running races, throwing things about." After a pause he added, "We had little religion in our family – my father hated the Church."

He was a man of faiths, this Father Rorty. He could not believe that his brother was still alive, yet he had faith that he might be. I came to see quite a lot of him that summer at Dobble's place, walking and talking with him. He escaped there gladly whenever he could from the necessities of his work – confessions, preaching, and so on – at the noisy rail-head camps down the valley. He lived by his faith, but I doubt somehow if he lived only for it. He had taken refuge in it from his family of brawling brothers. Now in a quiet place he liked to come out and walk in the sunsets.

He was moved by sunsets. We stood once on a point of that lake, lying east to west in a trough of the mountains. A canoe had just put off. At this time – it was in August – two tents were pitched across from Dobble's place, somewhat lower down the lake. A woman was there, on her way down to the railhead. A mountain whore stopped for a bit of business, travelling with her man and tent and stove in a "democrat" along the tote road by the railway track.

We watched the canoe go from us. The sun, low over the black rim of the western mountains, slanted on the lake waters until they became a carpet of creeping flame, failing as it advanced towards us, until at our feet only black water lapped, cold and spent and sobbing in the sandy runnel where the canoe's prow had rested. The canoe was wide, sat low in the water, two pairs of figures – four of Dobble's men – stooped monkishly against its centre thwarts, their backs to the west. The shape of the paddler in the stern rose above them, paddle flashing sword-like from the water and streams of water, blood-reddened against the sinking sun, running from its blade. For a long time we heard the tinkle of those falling paddle streams and the widening wake as a sigh upon the flaming waters. Then the four heads and the paddler's back and the canoe merged, blurred, became black and small and still, consumed before our eyes in the fiery expanse of lake and sky. As our vision faltered, the paddle flashed again, the lake's red bosom rose and swelled, and on it the black speck diminished to a quivering point of dissolution, hesitating one final moment at the fire-guarded gate of the world's end. Then we heard the canoe touch the other gravelled shore. We heard men's voices, and before us the sunset rode triumphant on the waters.

Of course Father Rorty knew where those men were going. His enemy, woman, was camped across the lake. But his thoughts, as it happened, were not on her.

He said to me, eyes narrowed against the red sunset, "Beauty and Truth, Truth and Beauty. But violence first. Beauty affronts the world by its violence. Its violence draws man and affrights him. Without the Cross our Saviour's life would not be beautiful. It is from His agony, not from His words, that the leaves of the poplar-tree are never still."

He continued, "My brother was a violent man. Perhaps out here in these mountains he learned something of the spirit's agony."

I was called back to look at one of our horses gone lame. I left the priest standing by the lake.

Later that evening Dobble came over to my tent. Beyond an odd meal I had refused his insistent hospitality.

He was in a state of high excitement. His bilious eyes bulged. His cheeks bulged. His moustache twitched. He chattered. He was swollen with his tidings.

"Do you know what's happened?" he asked.

"No."

"No, of course not. You wouldn't. How could you, after all? I didn't know myself until just now, this very evening, until I received the communication." His fretful yet exultant person suggested he might have just been reassured with a holy writ.

I told him to sit down on the blanket-roll.

"No, Mr. Denham, if you don't mind, I prefer to stand. . . . Mr. Denham, this place is becoming known. My work . . . my sign . . . bearing fruits. Mr. Denham . . . there is no one about? . . . I mean to overhear . . . this is all definitely confidential." I assured him we were alone. He swayed above me, his head of heavy hair close to the lantern hanging from the ridge pole. A man with tidings.

It appeared that Dobble had received a message, under "Value" brought to him by a brakeman off a work-train, from one of the company officials. "A man very high up," he went on, "someone who can do a lot for me. I know him well – we have met in Montreal. His name – you must know it; but that I am hindered from mentioning. You will understand my reticence."

It appeared further that a woman, accompanied by her maid, was making a pack-pony trip through the mountains. She had left Jasper with her outfit a few days before and intended to drop down to Yellowhead Lake from the Tonquin valley. On Yellowhead Lake she planned to camp for several weeks. Dobble had been asked to do what he could to make her stay a comfortable one. "You see the importance for me – for my work, Mr. Denham? Favour in the right places. I do not seek favours. Gentlemen merely return favours; and there is still the matter of the road and many other things to be settled. Do you see what I mean?"

He paused, then squatted beside me by the stove. His joints cracked as he let himself down. "It is my suspicion," he said, breathing heavily against my ear, his face a mask of shadow, "that there is more than would meet the eye between this woman and this . . . this railroad official. A relation – how shall I put it? To be frank, I suspect she is his mistress. Not that I would take advantage of such a situation, not for a moment. It is only necessary that he be aware of my knowledge, that is all."

I realised I was listening to an astute man – one whose astuteness, from the railroader's standpoint, was the more dangerous as he was not sufficiently astute to keep his mouth shut. Dobble's remark came back to me that the officers of the road had their brains in their bowels.

"Mistress?" I replied. "She may be his grandmother."

That, it seemed, was impossible. The woman had a foreign name, and the grandmothers of railway officials do not have foreign names, nor indeed do they travel by packhorse through the Rockies.

"And her name?" I asked.

"Ardith Aeriola," Dobble answered. "A lady," he added, "obviously a lady – and one of means." I was tempted to ask, "Whose means?" but refrained. Dobble was already beginning to appear to me as more than the simple being I had imagined him to be. It is too easy to put a man in a class and expect him to stay there. He carried a knife under his long black coat. He needed none of the weapons with which I might supply him.

I did inquire who was travelling with this woman through the mountains.

She had taken her outfit from Jasper, Dobble said. As well as her maid she had a cook with her and her guide – he pulled the paper from his pocket to consult it once more. "A man named Tay John," he said. "An odd name for a man to have." He wrinkled his brow, staring at the paper in his hand.

Dobble's small world at a cross-roads in the mountains was growing. It had a woman in it now – and Tay John, the yellow-headed hunter who had dismembered his arm that he might be as other men and travel with a horse beneath him.

I remembered the little priest with his doctrine of violence standing by the lake shore. Beside me was Dobble and his castle built of logs in the wilderness. I remembered, too, that woman was the death of heroes and the destruction of heroes' work – but heroes, those vulnerable men, are gone from the earth, and woman's power therefore no longer what once it was.

ELEVEN

The death of Father Rorty out there in the mountains brought forth much comment. The newspapers set about to explain it because it was essentially a happening beyond all their explanations. Nothing so arouses an editor as that. A chance to wonder. Some of you may remember the headlines at the time: "Mountain Priest Immolates Self," "Tragedy Enacted in the Rockies," and so on. His end was tragic, if you will, for he could feel the terror of his situation, and at the last, I have no doubt, realised there was no escape from the forces closing in upon him. He had time – time for that. Yet it was no voluntary humiliation. It began as that most haughty of adventures, a deliberate experiment in self-understanding.

I know, for he left something behind him. A letter, rather a long one. A letter to a woman. To *the* woman. To Ardith Aeriola. I found the letter and believe I was the only other to read it. "Miss Ardith" the men called her by that time. The letter, pressed between the pages of a small Spanish Bible, I found beside the trail when I was leaving Yellowhead Lake for the last time. In the Bible, too, was a very thin, leather-tooled note-book with the names and addresses of men in the East, in Montreal, New York, and overseas in London. Good addresses many of them. I looked into the envelope ripped open by a nervous hand, took the letter out and read it. For such things a gentleman can expect small pardon; but then I was – and still am – more interested in Ardith Aeriola than ever I was in being a gentleman. What's a gentleman? A fellow who uses the butter-knife when he's alone. The most you may expect of him is that he will never disappoint another gentleman. Still I have my code; and after I read the letter, although I kept it for a time to read it over again, finally I tore it up into small pieces and watched them float from me on a breadth of cold river water. Father Rorty's body had been brought down from the hills only a short time before. It was best that it should rest in peace. I was thinking of the woman, too. There were people, I knew, who, reading his letter, might have blamed her – oh, ever so carefully! – with all the indirectness of which self-conscious virtue, the virtue of those who have never been where the flames beat high, is capable.

Ardith – her very name would cause them to lift their eyebrows. And Aeriola – that was foreign, wasn't it? It sounded like a whisper in the dark. What was a woman with a name like that doing, alone among a crowd of men, on a barely known mountain lake? Yes, they would have shaped a case.

I knew no more than Dobble or the rest of them about Ardith Aeriola when she first came to Yellowhead Lake. Since then I have heard bits here and there – in Montreal among the railway men chiefly. In Winnipeg, too. She left bits of her story along her way as a mountain goat, down from the rocks, will leave white tufts of wool caught in the tough brush of the high meadows.

I think she found her name as she travelled. Aeriola – French, Italian? I am not sure – and Ardith might be anything at all. Hungarian was as close as I could come to her origin. It appeared that she had been born on the great plains of Central Europe, where the people wear for ever the unchanging ring of the horizon upon their shoulders. In the country on a small farm, she grew up among pigs and cows and chickens. Other houses dotted the sombre landscape, like burnt buns on a stove-top, and facing her always, wherever she might turn, the great blue distances with perhaps now and then a two-wheeled cart plodding along what seemed the world's edge, its driver and weary horse outlined against the sunset. She left there when she was sixteen. Why, God only knows. Because she was young, she was restless, she had a girl's dreams and feet to take her where they led. In a city of towers and narrow streets, she found work in a cabaret, one of those girls with black hair in tight white dresses who sit at tables and sip sweet drinks. It would be a hard life, with little money, and a room with a long-legged doll on a many-pillowed bed where she could bring such men she needed and who needed her. The next night, returning to the cabaret, she would collect the commission for the liquor consumed at her table. At any rate, after some years of this, she was a number at one of the better places in another town, singing peasant songs. A theatrical man from London heard her. He took her to England.

It would be closer to the truth, possibly, to say he saw her. It was her figure or the woman herself and not her voice that must have taken his eye, either that or he was a poor judge of what was wanted where he came from, because Ardith was not a success as a singer. One of the girls who came with her went on and made a name. But the story I heard was that Ardith was once hissed from the stage in the music-hall where she appeared – this, despite her grace, the undeniable appeal of her body, the sincerity with which she tackled the job of making those people like her. Someone shouted at her, "Lady, yer cawn't sing with yer buttocks!"

However, a chap with a handle to his name took her up. He made the mistake of bringing her with him to New York, for in New York she stayed. There was some sort of a scandal there – a prominent banker, likely in a white vest and a gold watch chain, was shot in her apartment. She was put on trial, to be cleared completely when a college boy confessed he had committed the murder from jealousy. She drew men to her, that woman, as she had drawn the interest of the theatrical man from London when he saw her in the cabaret. Not through anything you could put your finger on and say "Here it is." When you met her you felt you had found something. Reality of some sort – what that is no one ever knows in a world of make-believe. She had a presence – but it was her consciousness of that presence that gave her power. She was arrogant, as one is arrogant who comprehends her destiny and can meet it without fear or equivocation – and humble too, for she saw herself as well as those drawn to her, as the victims of that capricious and inscrutable force.

By now, of course, in New York, she was a woman mature beyond her years. Yet most women are that. To-morrow was the enemy past the gates. But it was to-day she lived – and to-day was a dagger against her breast.

In New York, too, her name had been in the papers because of the trial along with that of her titled English bene-factor – yes, they called him that. It was there in that sculptured city, in that outpost of man in time, in that white tombstone of the future, that she met the Canadian man of railways. He sent her west, promising to meet her there, or to call her east again, when the notoriety attached to her name had died away.

When I met her by Yellowhead Lake I recognised that, as they have it, she was a person to be reckoned with. She had a way of putting you at once upon your mettle. Perhaps it was her forthright manner of turning to meet you. She faced you fully. She stood silent, waiting for you to speak, to show cause for your being there at all. She stood very straight, so that she seemed taller than she was. She seemed actually to grow before your eyes. You did not question her. You would not question her, you felt, wherever you had come upon her – in a drawing-room, upon the stage, nor yet out there in the wilderness. She was a woman come to pass a few weeks, a month, by that green mountain lake. She and her maid, a young Spanish girl by the name of Juana, were the only women for miles around. It was all right. We accepted it as though it were the most casual of occurrences to have a woman drop down upon us from the hills. Whatever she did she did in her own right. She was a figure. She made her place. She stood for something – something vague, something not quite to be defined, like a woman on a barricade thrown across the street.

She was slight. She had black hair. A small face. Her eyes were dark. And when I say dark, I don't mean simply brown. They were black, so black that by comparison their whites showed slightly blue – fragile, clear as porcelain, so that you felt with a strong light behind her you might through them see the shadow of her being. Her lashes were short, thick, and when her eyes opened wide to stare at you in their unblinking way – as was her disconcerting custom – they linked themselves with the heavy line of her eyebrows. Her nose was fine and straight and her habit was to flex her nostrils ever so slightly while she listened. Her mouth was small, too, but the lips full and petulant. Her skin was browned, not so much from the sun as from a quality of its own. Her whole body, I knew, would be brown like that.

And you were conscious of her body, and of your own, all the while you were close to her. You would feel, as though for the first time, the rough wool of your trousers against the hair upon your thighs. You would feel the pull of the muscles across your chest. Remembrance would stir your flesh. You could not forget the woman in the clothes she wore. Ardith Aeriola wore a black riding suit – tight-fitting slacks instead of breeches, her small feet in riding gaiters. She liked to wear a red band around her hair – crimson, flaming red. She had a yellow blouse of silk – and from under it her breasts pointed. They were, I suppose, what made meeting her the challenge it always was. They were enough to cause a man to throw his hands in the air. They were the question waiting for its answer. Here was woman. Here was man's promise of immortality. Here was man's ease, and here, too, his torment. You might step forward, but her black eyes, piercing your hopes, would check your stride. She called you on, and your first submission was the signal for her denial.

Yes, she was a funny little piece – fierce, in an animal-like and panting sort of way; contradictory, exacting, submissive, defiant, and probably in the pride of her bearing showing her hate – and fear – of the world around her. I remember coming upon her one afternoon in a patch of green grass about half a mile from her camp. It was by the water, and tall fir-trees stood around. She was lying on the grass on her back, her knees doubled. She rolled slowly back and forth while she held folded in her arms against her bosom a young bear cub given to her by Joe Fournier, a trapper, working for Dobble. She was squeezing the cub, its back into her body, so that its bawling hindered the sound of my approach. Then I saw it reach back and with its pink tongue lick her chin. She gurgled and writhed the more upon the ground. The cub set to bawling again, its paws jerking in the air. That scene, her concupiscent attitude, had its aspect of passion, of the suffering, the struggle, that is passion's part. The cub saw me first, opened its mouth, sneezed. Ardith looked up.

She got to her feet at once, holding the chain attached to the bear cub's collar. "Oh," she said, in her husky voice, opening those eyes very wide, "I didn't know any-body" – she spaced the two words – "was *near*." Instinctively she ran very long, very neat fingers over the band holding her black hair in place. A fuzz of black hair was on her forearm. She panted. I glanced down at the cub. He was a little fellow, a runt, born in his mother's den the winter previous. He lay on his back, licking his forepaws.

"What's wrong with the cub?" I asked. "He doesn't stand up."

"His paws are sore. I guess they hurt him." I bent over, held him, looked at his forepaws and saw drops of blood upon the end of his toes. His nails had been cut off close.

"You cut his nails off?" I asked.

"Jim helped me," she said. Jim Hawkins was her cook from Jasper, a tall, bald-headed chap, hands bent with rheumatism, and his eyebrows singed from close attendance to his camp-fires. A flame worshipper. "Jim held him this morning," Ardith went on, "and I cut them off. He scratched me when I played with him."

"Oh," I said.

"See." She came closer to me. She pulled lower the open throat of her yellow blouse and exposed to me the rounded, the smooth, the warm and eager flesh of her breast. Not all, of course, but enough that I might see. "Come closer," she said, "and you can see." My hand reached out to touch the faint, inflamed line of the scratches.

She drew back. She laughed, showing small white teeth, crowded, sharp, unevenly spaced as a child's. The tip of her tongue lay among them like a snake's head on pebbles. She tilted her chin and regarded me from under lowered eyelids. "I said close, but not too close. To see, not to touch."

I swallowed.

"I understand," I said, "he scratched you. Still you needn't have cut his nails so close. You've cut them to the quick."

We stood looking for some moments at that deplorable little cub, tasting his own blood from the tips of his injured toes.

"I don't know what to do with him," said Ardith. "He won't eat. Sometimes he will lick the end of my finger when I dip it in milk. But he doesn't eat — and now he won't play."

"He misses his mother," I said.

"You think so — his mother, eh?" She hadn't thought of that. "You think I should send him back?"

"Where to?"

"To his mother, of course."

I pointed out that the she-bear was probably miles away in the mountains. The cub would never find her.

"Still I should send him back," she replied. "I will not be happy with him now. Tay John can take him back. He will know where to leave him."

"The cub can't even walk," I told her, "with those sore toes."

"Still," she said, "it is better so . . ."

Later that evening I saw Tay John, the cub in a sack on his back, climbing the hill behind Dobble's place.

He said, "She wants me to give him back to his mother. His mother, eh? Where is his mother, eh? No – he will only die. I take him back here a little way, then quick –" Tay John, grinning, drew his finger across his throat. "I'll kill him. He'll die easy."

Dobble, when Ardith arrived by the lake, seeing in her the opportunity to strengthen his hand against the railway, had put her up in a cabin he had rushed to completion. It was next to the one where Father Rorty stayed when he was not down at the railhead. Ardith, however, was not an early riser. The noise of hammers and of men shouting disturbed her. She had moved across the narrows to the north side of the lake by the railhead and had her tents put up there. Dobble, though disappointed, was not discouraged. His carpenters made a floor and wall for her tent and set up shelves inside it. His cook prepared special dishes and sent them, still steaming from the stove, across the lake in a canoe. Dobble himself ran about like a squirrel with a nut in its mouth, seeking something further he might do.

He need not have bothered. His men took it into their own hands. That rare creature, woman, was among them. They did not know, nor care, where she had come from. They saw in her, idealised, the image of all that they had left behind. Not to her, so much as to what she represented, they paid their homage. After work, in the long twilights, they went out on the lake and left the fish they had caught at her door. Jim Hawkins fried the fish for her. The men brought down blue grouse from the September hillsides. One of them killed a young buck, cut up the meat and tanned the skin for her use. An older man whittled, out of blocks of pine wood, groups of deer and bear and mountain goat, set them by her door one morning before she was up.

Tay John, it appeared to me, passed very little time with Ardith Aeriola. Indeed, he had put up his tepee across the lake from her camp and half a mile or so from Dobble's buildings. He explained to me that this was to hold his horses in good feed and away from the railway tracks. He had fifteen head with him. They made short work of the feed, and when I rode down from the upper Fraser where my surveyors had their work I had to set up my tent another two miles down the valley.

Tay John was a man not quite so tall as I remembered him from the afternoon in the valley above the Snake Indian country when he had outfought the grizzly bear. He had the build of a runner, deep chested, long muscled, lean. His yellow hair still swept his shoulders, bound by a beaded band back from his forehead and leaving on the collar of his buckskin shirt its dark stain of oil. From the stump of his left wrist, out of his sleeve, there showed a steel hook attached to a pad of leather which he had fitted to his forearm.

He still had the pinto horse left him by Alderson – but older now and already stiffened in the forelegs.

Tay John had become restless at having to stay a matter of weeks by Yellowhead Lake. His horses, too, the grass failing, were beginning to give him trouble, wandering up and down the valley of the Fraser. He wanted to be on his way, settled again in the routine of travel through the hills.

The activity at Dobble's place I believe appalled him. At first he sat for hours on a log watching the men at work. Then he withdrew – as if in dismay at the fuss and chatter over a project whose importance he failed to understand. He went back to his tepee, cooking his own meals, guarding his horses.

I passed by there one evening while he was standing outside the door, smoke from the fire within curling through the nest of poles at the tepee top. His legs were spread, each foot firmly set. Yet it was not an impression of solidity he offered, so much as one of emergence – from the ground itself, as though he had sprung up there a moment before my arrival. I looked to see the soil disturbed ever so slightly where his trim, high arched feet held their moccasins upon it.

We had met several times before to talk of horses, of grass, of his fight with the grizzly bear, to swap what we knew of the country.

Now as I squatted with him outside his tepee, and shared with him a swig of rum from my flask, he told me he was to take Ardith Aeriola and her maid over the high country to Mount Robson. The only one who knew the route, he had been hired by Brewster, an outfitter at Jasper, with whom the railway people had made arrangements for the trip. Tay John trapped in the winters, but for the last few summers had come into Jasper to work as packer and guide. He undertook the job only if they would send Jim Hawkins along as cook.

"Because," he explained to me, "Jim is a good cook. We have been out together before. But now something funny has happened. Miss Ardith says Jim is not a good cook. She says to fire him. She says the other woman with her will go, too, and wait at Jasper. She says, 'Tay John, you and I will go on alone and I will be the cook.'

"I say, 'No, Miss Ardith. That is work for someone who understands.' Then I walk away and she stamps her foot and calls me names."

"See," Tay John said, looking at me steadily, "I have been out on trips before. I am not a fool, a man like me must be careful. So I come over here to stay where it is quiet and no one tells me what to do."

A scar which might have been made by a knife-gash, or a claw, ran from the edge of his hair to his left eyebrow. From his excitement in talking, from the rum he had drunk, blood had run into it and stained it. Now as he talked it squirmed, grew and contracted, paled and became livid, angry and alive on his flexing brow, emerging from his yellow hair to fasten just above his eye. And through that hair, straight as if it had been pressed, I noticed a thin line of black, which, running back from the scar, gave the impression of a parting.

Slowly he said, "And the priest — surely some day I will kill him." He opened his hand, tensed his fingers, and regarding them, left his words framed in silence.

"Easy now," I said, "don't let anyone hear you say that. What's wrong with the priest?"

"I don't know what's wrong. I guess the sun doesn't shine on him. He takes her for walks and when she comes back she goes to her tent and cries. She is afraid of something he tells her. He says, 'Tay John, you should come with me. You should be a good man. You should pray.' He wants me to pray. He says to bend my knees. I know — he tells her this Tay John is a bad man."

Tay John, squatting on his heels, beat his fist upon the ground. His breath whistled through his nostrils. He got up and walked about.

"But — what is bad? That is why we stay here on this lake for three weeks and I chase horses all over the country. And he is afraid, too. The woman is afraid of wind, of high country, of a wolf howling. But he is afraid — I think he is afraid — of himself."

One evening Tay John told me he had waited in the bush by the side of the trail when Father Rorty was returning across the bridge from Ardith Aeriola's camp. "I made a noise . . . *grumph*, like a bear, like two bears fighting maybe, and the priest ran. He fell. He got up and ran again. He lifted up his skirts so that he could run faster. I see his white legs. Then I come out and I laugh, and when I laugh he is more afraid than before."

Tay John lay back and laughed. He threw a handful of soil into the air. Its pieces fell in his hair. "He was afraid . . . of nothing," he said.

I looked uneasily at Tay John, but his shadowed eyes told me nothing.

The next day blows were struck at Dobble's camp. A tall, tow-haired Swede stood on the unfinished log wall of the main building and pointed with his axe to Father Rorty, his head held down in thought, walking slowly back and forth by the lake shore. "Ya . . . a good yob he got," he shouted. "Voman drubble, dot's de madder."

A thick set French-Canadian rose up beside him. His fist flew like the hand of God. The Swede toppled off the wall. A crowd collected around him before he could get to his feet. Voices rose. I heard the name "Tay John." Someone said, "You leave the priest alone." Then Dobble appeared, and the group melted before the flurry of his arms.

These things, I suppose, might have drawn my attention more than they did at the time. It was not until a week or two later, when I came upon Father Rorty's letter, that their significance emerged. Before I destroyed the letter I re-read it several times. It was a letter to become a part of memory.

TWELVE

"Dear Ardith Aeriola," Father Rorty had written, each small upright letter so carefully formed that it might have been drawn, until at the end, when his hand grew weary, the handwriting tapered off almost to illegibility, "to-morrow morning before you are awake I will leave this letter inside your tent door. I will be passing there early for I am going up for a few days to Joe Fournier's cabin alone. Joe Fournier is a French-Canadian trapper who works here for Mr. Dobble. When I told him I was looking for some place where I might go to be completely by myself, he offered me his cabin. I will take some bacon with me and some bread. What else I require I will find there. The cabin is up on the top of that long spruce ridge you can see from your camp, running off the east slope of the Seven Sisters. There I will be able to look down on Yellowhead Lake. I will be able to see your camp-fire to-morrow night far below me in the darkness. I wonder how it will look so far away – or if perhaps I will be able to see it at all? So often we find as we go along that the very things we have most counted upon fail us. Without the sight of your camp-fire, warming me even at that great distance, I will be a very lonely man indeed, up there on the mountain top.

"Why should I go up there, to be lonely? You will understand because you are a woman – and more understanding
than other women, because you in your life have followed
your impulses to the end, until they have brought you to the
shores of this green mountain lake. Yes, you have heeded
the cries of your spirit. In that way you are a more spiritual
woman than I a man, for I have passed my life battling the
impulses rising within me. I am a man with a faith and am
bound to it, as Our Redeemer finally was nailed to His.
Perhaps a man with a faith is always a material man, for he
comes to prize too dearly the tangible symbols that hold him
and confirm him in his way. A priest who desires and has the
Love of God cannot be humble. Like all men of possessions
he comes to fear the outer world. He lets the cassock, that is
for his body, cloak his soul as well.

"He must do this if his faith is to survive. Saint Augustine
writes in his *Confessions*, 'the flesh lusteth against the spirit, and
the spirit against the flesh.' Yet I have wondered, since knowing
you, if to try to escape that is to deny the balance that life
imposes upon us. It has also been said that, 'it is the most just
punishment of sin, that each should lose what he uses not well.'
If that is so, am I not, dear Ardith, in danger of losing my soul?
Does not every priest lose his soul? Are we not really material-
ists, concerned more with the unanswered longings of our
bodies than with our souls? Is it not our bodies, robed in long
black, that we come to value, merely as symbols of what we are?
And restraint upon them becomes our great indulgence.

"I have spoken to you about this before. We discussed it
only this afternoon in our walk down by the lower lake, so that
my putting it down here will not be the shock it might otherwise be, coming from one who wears God's mantle in the

wilderness. For you have made me think. You have made me question the values I live by – not necessarily to renounce them, though always there is that peril – but to build them up again into something new and stronger, which, assailed by doubt, will thrive the more. That is the reason I go up to Joe Fournier's cabin. Up there alone on the mountain I may see a light, so awful, so stupendous, never before seen by man, that standing before it my shadow will make a trough in the ground behind me. It is not the possibility of that light I question. It is I who am before it. In *The Imitation of Christ*, a book I must give you, is written: 'He that knoweth himself, becometh vile to himself and taketh no delight in the praises of men.' So I have become – vile to myself. I go forth that I may be purified. A man is pure only when he believes.

"Where I stand now, I see two roads stretching before me, and neither can I see clearly. There are times when any man, even a priest, questions his vocation – when his soul emerges from the cassock. I have thought, and for this God's forgiveness I have already asked, that one night I would go down upon the lake shore, take off my robes, and leaving them behind me, plunge into the clean water and come out before your tent, a man. But that is fancy. What would I be on the other side of the lake – a poor shaking body, with no place in the world to go to. For I have no money. What could I do to live? And you – what would you do with this spirit, and its trembling mortal flesh, upon your doorstep? Would you laugh? Sometimes I think you would.

"You would laugh as you did this afternoon. Do you remember down by the poplar-trees with the lake behind you? I was on my knees so I could not see your face. My arms were around your knees. The warmth of your thigh was against my face. I tried to tell you then what was in me. I said I would leave everything I had and follow you. And in those minutes I would have done so. I would have walked into the mountains with you. I would have starved. I would have died gladly by your side. But you were wiser than I. You a woman, I a priest. You knew we could not go far. You looked over my head into the west, where the sun was setting down the valley, and you laughed, ever so lightly. You laughed, for I felt the tremor in your body. A little black-haired priest at your feet, what was that to you? Other, stronger men had been there before me.

"You have tempted me. 'Miss Ardith' is what the men about here call you. You have their tribute as well as mine. Yes, you have tempted me. You pull at my flesh, you call to my spirit. It is my flesh, and what I would have it represent, that has brought me to repentance. It is no sin to be tempted. Jesus Christ, Our Master, was tempted – but not by woman. It is in the victory over temptation that salvation lies. I see my salvation on the mountain-side above you.

"Mr. Dobble is your slave. Even Tay John, your Indian guide, has not escaped. I must get away from him as well. Familiar to me, yet strange is that man as if we had met somewhere before. I think of the many days you have been together on the trail, and deep in me a fire burns. I burn. I, a priest, who only this afternoon wanted more than anything else I could do to stand before you, a man, see another, who not abandoning the things he has made his life by, can do so without this sacrifice I fear to make. Yes, I fear. I fear the men about me. I fear the mountains – great waves of rock, tipped with foam, waiting to break upon me who walk in their valleys. I fear this cabin where I write to-night, my hand, shadowed by the candle, moving great upon the wall. Above me, the clock face, that exultant visage of for ever. I fear the rat that gnaws beneath my feet. More than that, my bones – I can feel his yellow teeth upon them.

"I had a brother once, as big a man as Tay John. He would have known what to do with you. He would not have put himself at your knees. He would not have written letters. He would have swum the lake or climbed the mountain to reach you. He would have taken you. But then, too, he would not have been a priest. Red Rorty would not have been a priest.

"But my writing, you will think, is endless. So it might be. But I must sleep. For six nights now I have not slept. There is sand behind my eyes. My head is full of the heavy sand of sleeplessness.

"Your face is too close for me to sleep. I have strange visions when I should be asleep – of flames, of water flowing, of a long white road.

"I leave you now. Some day, as you say, you may become a nun and go behind convent walls: I do not believe it will be so. But then you would know what it is to have a faith as your conscience.

"For now, pray for me – you cannot have forgotten after these many years. Whatever I learn, whatever is shown to me in that high solitude, I will be a better priest or a better man.

"How long I will be away I do not know. Five days or six, perhaps. What I will do afterwards probably matters little to you. Still I will see you when I return. One thing I ask at least – keep this letter, guard it well. Others would laugh at what is written here. I would be unfrocked. When I come back I will take it from you, tear it in small pieces and cast it on the lake. That lake, so deep, so sure, is you – I will leave my mark upon it.

"Dear Ardith Aeriola, I said I have repented. It is not so. I love you. For that I do not seek repentance. I seek only the gift of God's understanding. Will you listen to me when I return with that which I have found? That, while I am away, you may remember me, I put in the envelope a little crucifix of silver."

That was the end of the letter, signed "Thomas Rorty." Some of the words, as I have repeated them, may be mine – the gist is his.

So he went up from there, the little priest with the black hair, the blue eyes, and the sweat that would be beaded on his upper lip. One of the cook's helpers at Dobble's place saw him crossing the bridge in the blue light before dawn. He wore his cassock kilted to free his legs, and on his back he had a light pack – the bread, the bacon, perhaps his breviary as well.

It is a four hours' climb to Fournier's cabin. A well blazed trail marks the way. Father Rorty, unused to climbing, would take longer. I have been up there. Later it became a place men went to see. Dobble's men climbed up there on Sunday. It was not the place itself so much. It was the tree that was the thing.

I reached there one afternoon rather late and stood in the clearing at whose western limit was the low cabin, reminding me of a dog-house backed in among the spruce-trees. Spruce-trees lined the clearing on three sides, each tree, branches sloped to shed the winter snow, lifting its point against the sky, each tree bearing upon its crest the image of its perfect growth. From the cabin door I faced the west where the shafts of a sinking sun rolled the golden spokes of an ever-revolving wagon wheel across the sky. Close to me a creek, cutting the dark sward of the clearing, was a band of shimmering gold. At its western edge the clearing fell away, and there, raised against the heavens, was this tree. It was a pine. Long ago its trunk had been broken off by a slide or by the wind. Two stout branches had grown up instead, lightly tufted, to form a crotch. It was what the men there call a "school-marm tree." It stood sturdy, rather than tall, stark and black against the sunset. To me in those moments it had no phallic form. It was a figure, arms upflung.

Thousands of feet below was Yellowhead Lake, no longer green but now a slab of amethyst laid in the mountain rift – that amethyst to which an ancient people turned in hope from their intoxications. By the narrows were the carefully grouped buildings of Dobble's Lucerne, and across the water from them two tents where Ardith Aeriola stayed. By her tent a camp-fire burned. Above to the north was the black wall of the Seven Sisters whence the goats come down and leave their snow-white wool upon the bushes, and off to the south white-topped mountains, endless and glittering as a troubled sea.

I went to the clearing's edge and stood against that tree. Its crotch was somewhat higher than my head, but I held my arms along its arms. It moved against me with the wind. The branches above me sighed, the roots below me stirred in dark soil. There in that tree, against my body, pulsed the strength beyond all strength. I felt the earth, caught in the noose of time, lurch beneath me. The hum of stars was out beyond my finger-tips, for the arms of the tree in those moments were my arms, and its movements mine. I felt I was being lifted, my feet pulled from the ground. Our fathers worshipped trees. I think I understand.

Possibly Father Rorty, when he found himself alone in that lofty forest clearing, with the aspiring spruce-trees lined about him, did as I did. I don't know. Certainly the tree, apart from its fellows as he was apart from his, took his eye. He had eaten none of his food when they found him, so that it was the first evening of his solitude that he went towards it. He went to it with some ends of rope, filched from the old trapper's cabin. Climbing into the crotch he knotted two pieces around each of the arms, tightly to hold, yet loose so that he could force his hands between them and the tree. Around the lower trunk, where the stump of a branch remained about two feet from the ground, he hitched the other rope, looser this, but it was tightened when, hanging from above by his hands, he shoved his feet through the coil, his shoes removed, and crossed them one upon the other. He tied himself upon the tree. No one else was there to do it for him. No one was nearer to him than Yellowhead Lake, green and blue, far below, circled by the dark forest, and the knots were not the knots of a woodsman.

Still, the ropes held, for that was how they found him, Tay John and Joe Fournier, going up there for him when he had been gone a week and no word in the valley. In that tree, raised against the sky, he, a priest, had seen yet another symbol – the symbol of the Cross. "For one night," he thought, "I will lie upon the Cross. I will take this cross of doubt, so heavy on my shoulders, and place myself upon it. I will lift myself higher than any man before me, except Christ Himself, has been lifted. I will know the secret of the Cross. I will gaze out upon the world, secure in my suffering above it."

Priestly arrogance could go no farther.

He must have worked feverishly, consumed with the splendour of his idea, and smiled at the sweat from his labour. Perhaps he was happy then, when he saw his shadow and the tree's shadow, spreading over the clearing to the forest edge. Immense it went beyond. The shadow of the Cross was over all the world, and men bent beneath it. The twilight faded. Under the tree-roots, the ground sucked in shadows and spewed up darkness. Night rolled in a wall over the continent and behind it, people caught in the slow violence of sleep, as though some sickness had come upon them, lay littered across the countryside. Rivers would still run, wind would blow in darkness – but behind him he felt a light. If he could turn his face he would see it.

Stars shone for a time. The Big Dipper wheeled above him. Then clouds came and with them the rain. It touched his brow, cool and fresh as salvation. He heard it on the cabin roof. He heard it pit the ground and patter on the willow bushes. It swirled in eddies over the forest. It wet his throat, and water coursed down his back when his head fell forward. Later the wind blew, and he tasted wet snow bitter on his lips, for this was a cold September storm. He shook. His arms ached. The ache of his body rose as a great sound within him. He feared, and longed to go down to the ground again. He moved his hands to loosen them from their binding. No feeling was in his fingers. His wrists had swollen and the rope about them, shrunk with the rain, cut into the flesh. He was impaled upon the tree like time upon the hour. He opened his mouth to shout and snow fingered the back of his throat. Wind took his breath and hurled it from him. He sobbed. Froth flew from his mouth, white in the night.

It rained. It snowed. It blew. For three days the storm lasted. At Dobble's place, outside work was stopped. Ardith Aeriola came over to warm herself by the cook-stove. Men spoke of the priest up there alone on the mountain-top. Then the storm broke. The sun came out. Eyes winced before the glare of snow melting on the hillsides and on the rocks above.

Four days later Tay John and Fournier set off afoot up the mountain to see what had become of Father Rorty. They found him. He was naked as Christ. Froth was still upon his lips, and the long forelock of black hair wavered in the wind across his sun-scorched forehead. The arms upon that tree were still outspread, waiting to embrace the world, and the naked feet hung yearning for the soil. A hawk circled over-head. Bright-eyed marten had come from the forest, climbed the tree, and eaten into the soft flesh of the belly.

Tay John carried down the body wrapped in canvas upon his shoulders. "The little priest is light," he said, "like a boy. Now he is afraid no more." They put him in a pine-box and shipped him back to Edmonton for burial.

"Mr. Denham," Dobble said to me, "he went up there to kill himself, to commit suicide upon that tree. It is fantastic. It is unbelievable. I doubt my eyes."

So I thought myself until I read the letter the priest had written, when he spoke more than once of his return. I remembered the rain would shrink the ropes till he could not escape.

I wonder now, thinking of the priest, tied upon the school-marm tree, when he was dying, when he was in the wild delirium that may have come before his end – what was before him: the shape of the Cross, the vision of his faith, or the face of the woman – pale, round, close and real as the moon that stared him down? Or up there, so high above the earth, was there only the sound of the wind blowing, and far away the sound of running water where men who thirst may drink?

THIRTEEN

Father Rorty, naturally enough, was for a long time the back-log of our conversation. Men's talk would return to him, seeking comprehension. They would look up from their work at the lofty ridge, blue with its spruce-trees, rising from the lake's far shore, point with a hammer or an axe, then drop their heads once more to their tasks. Already they had named it "The Priest's Mountain." What had happened there increased their awareness of their fellow man, brought them somehow closer together and at the same time estranged their understanding. Who could tell what were the thoughts of the man lifting the other end of the log upon his shoulders, of the one up there nailing shingles on the roof, even of the cook lost in the toil of his pots and pans? Without their recognising it, the riddle of human destiny was propounded to them, and the shadow of a common lot fell upon all alike. It remained for Dobble to adopt what he called "a realistic view."

"No one regrets more than I, Mr. Denham," he said to me, patting the ends of his moustache with his thin, tobacco-stained fingers. For an instant, the backs of his hands outward, his elbows close to his sides, standing tall and lean, sallow-faced, against the log walls of the building, he assumed a foreign dignity – yes, he appeared to me a stranger, a man with truths to impart – a stranger is always that. "No one regrets more than I," he repeated, "that Father Rorty is no longer with us. He was a good man. Yet we live in a world of facts, you and I – and I take a realistic view of all these things, their significance. Do I make myself clear?"

"By no means," I said.

Dobble squinted his copper-flecked eyes against the sun.

"Well, Father Rorty's death now. What has been its effect – I mean so far as my development here is concerned?"

I shook my head.

"Come, come, Mr. Denham. You are a man of discernment. I hardly feel I need point out to you, that by now the story will have appeared in the newspapers from coast to coast. Yellowhead Lake will be mentioned. Lucerne, this work of mine, as well. People will ask questions. Most of them will have heard for the first time of this part of the Rockies. It will be a means of getting the region known. Publicity is the word, Mr. Denham." Dobble hatched a cigarette from his case and poked his neatly booted foot at a pile of shavings.

"Now, do you see?" he asked, blowing a cloud of smoke through his pursed lips. "It's as clear as that smoke to me. One can't avoid these . . . what should I say? . . . implications . . . however unfortunate may be the causes that give them rise."

I admitted the force of what he said, not omitting to point out, however, that in my opinion such publicity even if obtained might serve only to give the Yellowhead country notoriety rather than a reputation drawing people for the summers. Dobble was a growing puzzle. He could not fairly be called blind to facts, except in so far as those facts threatened the beliefs that gave his life impetus. That of course is the hazard of belief. It is necessarily a form of intellectual myopia. Dobble, when I knew him, had staked his whole future on Yellowhead Lake. He distrusted any logic which might cast doubt upon it. He would not listen to reasons nor to reason. "I tell you, Mr. Denham," he once said, "we are standing on the threshold of a new era. A new era. Men of vision have made this country of the west. Only men of vision, of vision, mind you, can see that what is already done is but a beginning.

"This railway — what will be its consequences? I will tell you. Where Edmonton is to-day a city of a few thousands, in ten years, no less, you will have a city of hundreds of thousands. Winnipeg, Saskatoon, Moose Jaw — these will be the metropolises. I am out here because I realise what this is going to mean. There will be a new leisure class in the west. They will look to the mountains as Europe looks to Switzerland. Yes, a Switzerland."

He came forward and tapped me on the chest — my chest bore the brunt of his ideas. "You think I should have commenced on a smaller scale. You have said so. My only worry is, Mr. Denham, whether or not I have begun upon a scale sufficiently vast. Vast, that's the word. By next summer I will be able to accommodate two hundred people here. But what is that? Nothing. A beginning, no more. I will put chalets all through these mountains. A fortune in it for the right man. When I consider what lies before me, I cannot sleep. I get up from my bed and pace the floor. I can *see* those people waiting out there beyond the foothills — horses, motor-cars, roads, hotels . . . time, so short . . . two years or three to prepare . . . You will see, you will regret your decision not to throw in your lot with me."

I became accustomed to such outbursts as that. So far as he went, he spoke the truth. He actually did see hordes of tourists clamouring for admission to the mountains. Time was treading on his heels. That he saw forty years ahead instead of two or three made no difference to him. It was futile to insist big cities are not born overnight and that it was the function of a railway, which would profit from the haul, to invest in large mountain hostelries, and not a risk for an individual to take beside a scarcely known lake in the Rockies. New York was five days away. There was no Paris overnight from the Rockies, nor a London twenty hours away, as was the case with Switzerland. The belief that the prairies would provide their equivalent was essential to Dobble's illusion, and to that belief he clung. How much money he ventured and lost without his idea being put to the test, I am not the one to say.

The Aphrodine Girdle – I would not expect its name, much less its use, to be widely known. Certainly I had attained a certain sort of maturity without knowledge or experience of either.

Lucerne, of course, was taking on form. Some twenty cabins, their freshly peeled logs bright against the pines behind them, lined the road down to the lake. Above them, raised a bit on the hill slope, was the main building, now called The Lodge, with a high raftered roof over its hall and a great stone fireplace built into its wall. Off to one end was the dining-room. Beyond that again, the kitchen. Furniture, still lacking, was to be made by hand from the natural woods of the forest. To the western end of the hall, up a few steps, was Dobble's office.

One morning, not long after Father Rorty had been brought down from the mountain-top, I drifted in there to pass the time of day with him before leaving for my last trip of the season up the Fraser. I was to return with the surveyors, their tents and equipment, to the railway, load them on a freight train and then trail my horses back to Jasper. Dobble, as it happened, was not in his office. On his wide desk – an enormous affair for the place – set by the window was a slip of paper, a leaflet. Littered with black type, it reminded me of a theatrical announcement. Stepping out for a moment he had left it there. Afterwards when I told him I had dropped in he said he had been called out suddenly, very suddenly. Someone had dropped a cigarette on a pile of shavings in one of the cabins, a fire had threatened. "The whole place might have gone up in flames," he said.

As the leaflet seemed in no way confidential, I turned it about to read it, letting it lie there on the desk-top. In large letters across the top were the words, "*The Aphrodine Girdle.*" Then in smaller letters underneath, "*Recommended for all men, young and old. Trial free of obligation.*" The rest was in smaller letters, and I passed it over. I turned the slip back to where I had found it.

I went out. I was embarrassed – affronted by the utter invincibility of the man's illusions, by his vanity. Vanity, vanity . . . the fat upon the spirit.

Of course I had heard that Dobble had been running after Ardith Aeriola, his tongue fairly hanging out. The few favours he had done her, he considered to be ample assurance of her submission. Still his progress had not been marked. She held him well at arm's length.

Pete the blacksmith told me something of what was going on. A short, thickset fellow with a cap of sun- and forge-browned baldness on the top of his head, deep-set eyes, beetling eyebrows, and the bristles of a luxuriant moustache poking into his nostrils, so that often he would interrupt himself to sneeze. Pete and I had had many consultations on shoeing horses. Twice during the summer he had shod mine, and we still differed as to whether, as he said, they should be shod long, or as I said, short for the mountain trails.

"Horses," he said once to me, looking up from his anvil, "be damned to them. Shoes for horses – give me a place on a mountain high up. Mount Robson, now, there's a peak for you. Give me a forge up there, and I'll make slippers for all God's angels. Gold ones I'll make for them, and you'll see them twinkling flying off into the sunset."

Then he laughed and tapped his hammer on the iron. "Yes," he said, "all God's angels shod. That would be a man's job. Golden slippers. You know, Mr. Dobble gave me that idea. He brought that Miss Ardith down here once. He said to her, 'Some day I'm going to have Pete make you a pair of slippers, gold ones, like the angels wear.' She said, 'Angels don't wear no slippers. They got wings. Anyway,' she said, she was wearing a dress that day, 'anyway,' she said, 'I like the ones I got on.' She pulled up her dress and put her foot out till we could see her knee: Black stockings – it was sure a pretty knee. I thought for a minute he was going to get down and kiss it. He almost came to pieces lookin' at it."

"Still, at that," Pete finished, "I don't see why she don't go for him more than she does. He's got money. He's a gentleman, ain't he? Tay John ain't got nothin' but his yellow hair and the horse he rides on. A horse now, you understand a horse, but women –" Pete shook his heavy head over women.

It was the first week in October, on a Sunday, that two weeks later I came down the Fraser. My surveyors went away with their outfit on the train. The next day I was to follow with the horses into Jasper. That night, at dusk, I went up to Dobble's main building. The men were to be there, and Ardith Aeriola. She was leaving in a day or two for the East. It was a house-warming to mark the completion of the main part of the season's work at Dobble's place.

In those days I kept a tent set up near where I let my horses run. I had been coming down often during the summer – to fetch new supplies and mail for up the Fraser. Behind my tent, buried in the ground, the top soil covered over with pine needles, I had a gallon of rum. I was often wet, and always tired at the finish of my fifty-mile ride down the river to Yellowhead Lake. This Sunday night, before starting up to Dobble's place, I emptied down my gullet what was left in the jar. I drank a few silent toasts under the trees to the summer that was past and to the others coming down the years.

As I walked up I bent my head against the east wind. I smelt snow in the air. It was cold. In the wind the tall pines bowed, tossing their plumed branches, creaking and groaning in their torment. "Ah," said the forest. "Oh," said the wind. "I'll blow," said the wind, "till I loosen your roots in the ground, till I blow the needles from your branches and the branches from your stems. After me winter comes, to lay its snow and silence on the land, on uprooted trees, on the grasses and the moss, on the frozen waters, on the paltry buildings man has built." Yes, winter was over there beyond the mountains.

I stood a few moments before Dobble's main building, light from lanterns and candles streaming from its windows, tilted on the hillside, like some ship foundered in a strange and hostile sea. Behind the logs, out of the storm, man moved, secure for a while from the elements around him. The murmur of voices reached me. Storms might come, but they would pass away. Winter would come, but it would bring its spring. Men would die, but children would come after them, lifting up white faces to the light. Man's voice, sustained by its own echoes, rolled on in murmurs, in shouts, in laughter, in weeping, in exhortation and prayer, in whispers, hoping somehow to be heard, pausing now for an answer – rising again to drown dismay when no answer came, drifting across the vasts he walked. Man was alone. The future was the blind across his eyes. He held his hands before him, to feel. He listened to the seconds, ticking, measuring his mortality, theirs the only sound in all eternity where suns flamed and stars wheeled and constellations fell apart.

A woman's laughter reached me from the building. I shook myself. After all I stood in rutted soil where men had laboured. The buildings they had made were before me. There were smooth logs that I might touch. A door I might enter. Liquor that I might drink.

Liquor . . . I entered, pushing the door to against the wind. Dobble took me by the arm, brought me to his office, poured me a drink of whisky. I may have had two, or three, I don't remember. I remember well the man strutting before me, a cock in his own back yard.

"How old do you think I am, Mr. Denham?"

"Haven't the least idea."

"Well, make a guess . . . how old do you think?"

I made a guess. I said forty-four.

"Ho-ho," he said, wavering back and forth. "Forty-four, eh? Forty-four, is that all? You'll never guess. A young man still, Mr. Denham, with his life before him – and something behind him, too. Lucerne – the greater part of my work here, the hard part is behind me. Achieved. Achieved, that's the word." He was silent for a moment, then winked a blood-shot eye in solemn wisdom. "I never felt younger in my life," he said.

"How many drinks have you had?" I asked.

He waved a lofty hand. "Not too many, you may be sure."

But there was more than liquor in him. What I can only call a misguided exuberance. He slapped his narrow chest and almost knocked himself off his feet. His long coat-tails swung.

He coughed. The preposterous fellow was probably wearing his Aphrodine Girdle around his wasted loins. Around his head it might have done some good. That was where rejuvenation was needed.

"Youth," he said to me, "that's the thing. To feel young. We treat God, Mr. Denham, as though he were an old man. If he is a god you may depend on it, he's kept himself young. A young fellow with a girl on his lap and not much time to attend to other business.

"Have another drink," he said, "it's good stuff. Got it for to-night especially."

He came close to me.

"I have approached Tay John," he said.

"What!"

"Yes. I am trying to come to an agreement with him. I want him to be here next year to meet the trains."

"To meet the trains? Tay John meeting trains?"

"Tourists, Mr. Denham. Think of the impression. Tay John on the platform to meet them when they get off the train. A man of the country – the sort of thing they've read about, and dressed in skins, of course."

"Well, my bet is," I said, "that first you'll have to capture him. Then you'll have to stuff and frame him. After that you might be able to set him up on a station platform."

Dobble wagged his finger under my nose.

"Don't be too sure. He is open to suggestion."

"What did he say to you?"

"He said nothing. But he did not openly oppose the idea. He left me with the feeling that he would be amenable." Dobble turned suddenly about to face the door. He listened as though fearing an intrusion. He faced me again. "The trouble just now is," he said, "the woman – this Ardith Aeriola. She has him under her thumb." Dobble pushed his thumb upon his desk, as if driving in a tack. "You mark my words, there is more happening there than meets the eye."

"Come, come," I replied, "he's been staying over on this side of the lake away from her. She has her maid, and the cook. . . ."

"The cook has been fired," Dobble assured me. "He went back to Jasper to-day. She had her way about that at last . . . and the maid, I suspect, will be going to-morrow or the next day."

"Nonsense – Ardith Aeriola herself is going back east in a few days, or so I have heard."

"Mark my words," Dobble repeated, "she may not be going east for some time yet. My suspicion is that she is going to have Tay John take her off alone on this trip over the mountains to Mount Robson. That is her plan. I know. I have an eye for such things."

He paused, as if he had lost his wind.

"Do you see what I mean?" he insisted. "Tay John has his place. It is here, where he can be used. His appearance . . . It is not out on the trail alone with a woman . . . a woman after all for whom I feel a certain responsibility. I have urged him to begin work with me now, to-morrow. I told him he would have nothing much to do until next summer. But I offered to look after him, to feed him. I am not a man of scruples, Mr. Denham, but there are certain things at which I balk."

"Tay John, then, wouldn't begin work immediately?"

"He wouldn't say. He remained silent. He did not blink an eye. It was like addressing a totem pole. But he did not dissent. I pointed out to him that if this Miss Ardith was going away he was free. But you see, he is bound to her . . . bound!"

I told Dobble I thought imagination was playing him a trick.

"Tricks!" He slapped the palms of his hands together. "Bah!" he said.

We went out into the big hall. The light of many lanterns lashed my eyes. I opened them to the sting of smoke, pipe smoke, cigarette smoke, smoke blown by the wind down the chimney of the fireplace. Someone was playing an accordion. Standing on the steps leading down from Dobble's office, I looked over the heads around me. About thirty of his men were in the room, faces tanned and lined with sun and wind. Freshly washed, foreheads gleamed white. A few of the men wore white celluloid collars with ties. There were shirts the colour of blood, the blue of the sky, the green of grass. It was movement and tumult. Liquor hummed in my head. Noise in itself will blind a man. Of what was around me I caught only flashes here and there – as in a thunderstorm when briefly under the lightning the countryside is revealed, trees standing, a glimpse of a river still flowing, a horse on a hillside, tail sucked between his legs.

Dobble stepped jauntily towards Ardith Aeriola. She was by the fireplace, eyes bright, though faint half-circles sallowed the skin beneath them. She wore a silver crucifix at the throat of her black dress. Juana, her maid, rosy cheeked, face split by a laughing mouth so that she resembled one of those lanterns you see on Hallowe'en, had several men around her. They came as close as they dared to the peril of woman in their midst. Off in a corner, alone, standing straight and still as if he had been set there and forgotten, was Tay John. He was watching Ardith through half-closed lids, intent as one who stares into distance. I recalled Dobble's image – Tay John was the totem pole, the unmeasured quantity at the gathering.

"Ah," Dobble said, bending stiffly at the waist before Ardith Aeriola, "like a star, always changing, but always shining."

"Stars, Mr. Dobble, and shining – a night such as this?" Outside the wind blew its mighty trumpet.

"A figure of speech, Miss Ardith. Nothing more. Merely a rough attempt to pay my compliments to a beautiful woman – and also, if I may say so, to the stars." He put his hand under her arm. They moved to a window. I suppose he wished to find out about the stars.

I talked for some time to Pete the blacksmith. He was off again with his angels and their golden slippers – when it happened.

It was the crack of an open palm on flesh.

"Jesus! Did you hear that?" asked Pete.

It cracked across the room. Men disowned the words they had been speaking, left them hanging in mid-air, swallowed in the stillness, as they turned their heads. There by the window were Ardith Aeriola and Dobble. He was standing back from her, hand to his cheek, his back a bit towards us. He turned to us his face, suddenly haggard, his long hair hanging down over his ears. He was pale, his long body bent, his stomach indrawn, as though in pain – the pain of age.

"Keep your dirty hands off me," Ardith cried in a voice pitched to scream. "Juana!" she called to her maid, "Juana! Come here quick!" Juana went to her side, her long skirt trailing on the floor, hiding her feet, so that, her face upturned, she seemed to be running on her knees.

I guess Dobble did not know, or had forgotten, that no woman so respects the conventions as one who lives hazardously beyond them. Carried away by his own exaltations he had chosen the wrong place, the wrong time. He stood now between the scorn of woman and the ridicule of men.

"Oh," he said to her, "so that's the idea, eh? You're putting on airs?" Knee pockets in his baggy trousers, he looked as if he were about to jump.

The little cross glimmered at Ardith's throat. It bounced with her heart-beat. Her bosom rose and fell as though she had climbed a long hill and stood at last on its top. "A gentleman . . ." she said.

"What do you know about gentlemen?" Dobble blurted out, "until you see them undressed? A railroader's tart . . ." Before he could finish she stepped forward. She slapped his face again, twice. Blood showed on his long yellow teeth. "You . . . you . . . you goat face," she said. "You and your gentlemen undressed. Gentlemen? *Pouff!* Who ever saw one without his trousers?"

Dobble pulled his handkerchief out of his sleeve, shook it and dabbed his mouth. "Don't like me, eh? But eat my food, accept my favours . . . I'll show you who's boss around here." I was about to move in between them, when he lunged forward, pulled her to him and pushed his face against hers. She beat his head, his shoulders with her fists. Tears of anger shone in her eyes.

Before I could move I was shoved aside. For an instant the broad mackinaw-checkered back of Tay John was in front of me. Then I saw Dobble literally lifted from his feet. With his one arm Tay John held him above his head, hair, coat-tails and arms flapping, before he flung him on a wicker chair against the wall. The chair collapsed and, stunned, Dobble fell to the floor.

I heard Ardith shout, "Come, Juana, we are going." The door opened and shut and they were gone. It had come about so quickly that we were left in a half-circle staring at a closed door. But when Tay John went towards it, Dobble's men were upon him. All of them tried to lay their hands upon him, to pull him down. "The yellow-haired bastard," said Pete, rushing by me, "does he think he can throw the boss around like that!" He shouted, "Let me get at him!"

For a long time the yellow head stayed by the door. It moved back and forth as though tossed by the wind. I watched the fight from its edges. I could not get near to help him, nor yet, as I well might have done, carried away by the intoxication of the crowd, to help pull him down. Johansen the Swede was in there. Pete, the blacksmith from the prairies; Scottish teamsters, French-Canadian axemen. Tay John was assailed by all at once. It was not only what he had done to Dobble. It was what was different in him – the heritage of his ancestry, the challenge of his hair, which gave fury to their assault. That fury would pull him down, change his shape, make him one with those who fought against him. He stood alone, above them, pushed and pulled, his face beaten till blood sheened and smoothed his chin. They didn't get him down. His back to the wall, he kicked and struck, broke from their hands, turned again to confront them. "Hold him. Let me hit him," someone shouted. I heard a chair smashed and a thud. Pete came back, a cheek streaming with blood. "Look what that son-of-a-bitch did with that God-damned claw of his," he cried.

Finally Tay John twisted from their fingers, broke away, slipped through the door. One of the men remained standing in a dazed fashion gazing at some yellow hair clutched in his fist. He shook his head, opened his fingers. The yellow hair floated to the floor, was picked up and carried along by the wind from the opened door, scuttling as if on small, unseen feet, until it settled by the steps leading up to Dobble's office.

They chased Tay John into the dark, lost him in the bush. "Like a bloody deer. You couldn't catch him," a young red-headed Scotsman, a gash from a broken branch above his eye, said when he returned. "But we pulled down his tepee for him," he finished proudly. "Laid it flat on the ground."

I looked about that place of overturned benches and tables, smashed bottles and blood-spattered floor. I went into Dobble's office. It was empty.

I found my way along the trail and across the bridge to Ardith Aeriola's camp.

Through the canvas wall of her tent a lantern hung from the ridge pole, pulsed and glowed, a heart beat in the darkness. I lifted the door flap. Inside one of the beds spilled a flood of crimson blankets. On its edge Tay John sat, head hanging between his knees. From his brow great drops of blood dripped to the floor, staining it in sudden, separate splotches as if through the white-pine boards at his feet rosebuds burst and bloomed.

As I entered he turned his head, regarding me with a brown eye, enigmatic as a bird's, with no focus my own could catch. He sighed, dropped his head again.

Beyond him Ardith let fall her black, silken skirt, lifted to reveal the moulded beauty of her sallow thigh. In her hand she held a white strip ripped from her petticoat.

Seeing me, she stepped back, fingers at her mouth, to suppress a cry. She did not speak, but instead moving cautiously forward, put her hand on Tay John's shoulder. She bent low, began to wrap the bandage about his head, hers close to his own, and her lips against his yellow hair as though she whispered. A vein stood out in the dead centre of her forehead, making a ridge from her nose into the part of her thick black hair.

"I'm sorry," I said, "I dropped in to see if I might be of help, not to intrude."

She shook her head. Her lips shaped the word "No!" She caressed Tay John's cheek, urging him closer to her. She uttered no word, fearful that mere sound would break the tie that held him. At her man's side, she stood on guard. It was as though his thick shoulders between us were in dispute.

Before her Tay John's head, bound in white surrender, was bowed, his right arm folded on his knee, the left, with its hook of steel, hanging helpless from his shoulder.

I waited no further answer. I did not turn. I backed into the night, quietly, raised upon my toes.

In the cook-tent, farther in the trees, another light was burning, low to the ground, a candle on a block of wood, where Juana, the maid, kept watch.

Returning to the bridge, and only a few yards from it, I was startled by deep breathing, the crack of breaking branches in the bush to my right. I thought of a bear, of a moose charging out of the dark. It is not darkness man fears. It is his helplessness before eyes which see when his own are blinded.

I hesitated. The sound did not approach, nor go from me.

I called, "Who's there?"

"Is that you, Mr. Denham? I'm off the trail." It was Dobble's voice. Somehow I was reminded of the biblical sacrifice – the ram caught in the thicket.

I went in there and brought him out.

"I became confused," he explained.

"It's pretty dark to be out," I said, "unless, of course, you have business."

"That is exactly what I have . . . business." He drew himself up before me. The black cloak he was wearing, falling to his knees, the wide-brimmed hat, even then when I had to lean forward, to peer to make him out, gave Dobble an air — the air of one on a mission of secret hazard.

"Down there." He waved his arm to the trail towards Ardith Aeriola's camp. He was beginning to feel the liquor he had drunk — and the movement threatened his balance. I reached out to steady him.

"Come along with me," I said. "It's late. Time to turn in."

"Mr. Denham, my mind is made up. I am resolved. I am going to put an end to this . . . this business once and for all. I know quite well what is taking place and I am going to stop it."

I tried to take him with me. He shook me off. Robed in his purpose, the Aphrodine Girdle about his middle — and for its efficacy I at that moment would have been impelled to speak — Dobble left me. He ran a few steps. He tripped over a stone, over a newly flung spider web, or perhaps merely over his own intentions. He lurched, gasped, coughed, stumbled again. On all fours he made his way towards the glowing lantern throb of that tent from which in vain I called him back.

FOURTEEN

Before anyone stirred in Dobble's camp I awoke, gathered in my horses, and was on my way to Jasper, driving the horses before me along the trail lightly covered with snow. Headed towards their home range on Henry House Flats where, half-starved, they would wait the winter out till needed again in the spring, they ran before me with little trouble. My second packer, with all the camp equipment and saddles, had gone in on the freight the day before.

The bars were down as I crossed the bridge over the narrows of the lake. Someone had been by before me. What horses there were, or how many, I could not see because their tracks were obscured by the fifteen head I drove. I passed Ardith Aeriola's two tents. A long jagged tear was in the back canvas of one of them. I wondered a bit at that. The snow and wind would enter there. A mile or so farther on I dismounted to pick up a small book lying in the snow by the trail's side. It was a Spanish Bible, its covers closed with a button. I put it in my pocket. It belonged, I supposed, to Ardith or to her Spanish-speaking maid. I might have turned back to leave it in her tent, but if I stopped, my horses, nicely strung out with an old mare in the lead, would have scattered all over God's creation. I would leave it for her in Jasper, where she could pick it up on her way east. Somewhat farther on I observed where three horses earlier that morning had turned off the trail towards the Priest's Mountain. I knew then, I had what we call a feeling – she had been before me and dropped the Bible as she rode. Instead of returning east she had gone farther into the mountains. Into the snow and the cold. With Tay John? Dobble had been right. Perhaps. I would not be sure.

I took the Bible from my pocket and opened it. Just within its cover was the thin leather note-book with the addresses and names of men in eastern cities. Even as I rode, bouncing in my saddle, a perfume, faint as remembrance, rose to my nostrils from its pages. Had it fallen from her, or had she discarded it, left it behind as a gesture, as that for which she had no further use? I tied my reins around the saddle-horn. Well in the Bible's middle, pressed between the pages, was the envelope, her name written upon it, with Father Rorty's letter. My curiosity got the better of me. I read it. Arrived in Jasper I read it again. I tore it up and threw it away on the river. Father Rorty would have had it thrown on the lake – a symbol. But a river, too, is a symbol – it flows on, and the memory of Father Rorty will flow on.

I was in Jasper only a night and a day before taking the train into Edmonton. While I was there Sergeant Ignatius Flaherty, of the Mounted Police, was called to go to Lucerne. "There's been some trouble up there," the station agent informed me. "They want a doctor, too."

Of course, I was interested in what the trouble might be, and by then had my own ideas regarding it, but my interest was not sufficient to hold me in the small mountain town. In

Edmonton I saw no newspapers for several days. I was too much taken, maybe, with the labels on whisky bottles. Good reading that, for one who has been the whole summer and part of autumn out on the trail. However, in a way that stories have, it tracked me down. For a while it was the talk of the town. Men stood around it, sopping up its details, as they would stand around a bowl of punch. They generally agreed that Dobble had got "what was coming to him." During his visits to town they had heard a lot about Dobble and of what he was doing – from Dobble himself.

"To hear him talk, you'd think he was making over the mountains," one of them said to me. "Building a few cabins around a lake. What does that amount to I'd like to know?"

"Anyway," another one said, "I wouldn't care to be in his boots now. He won't want to show his face here for a time, if I know anything."

I went to the bother of going round to the local office of the North-West Mounted to find out what I could about it. The inspector there, a man by the name of Jay Wiggins, as I entered was seated at a small desk in the corner of the room. He was flanked on two sides by shelves of blue-backed reports, and sat there, head bowed, hands clasped upon the desk-top, as if in reverence before the accumulated and recorded achievements of the Force. At first all I saw was the oval of his wiry black hair, dipped short so that the white of his scalp showed through. He lifted up his head wearily. His eyes, shielded by heavy, yellow lids, were no more than half opened, but regarded me with such unwavering intentness that I soon became uneasy. I found myself rubbing my hand across my face, coughing, scuffling my feet on the floor – anything to break the spell of that steadfast stare. His face, clean-shaven except for a small brown moustache like a clip on his upper lip, gave an impression of greyness from its beard's stubble; and his forehead, broad rather than high, was creased with horizontal furrows. His shoulders under his red tunic were broad, too, remarkably broad and powerful. As he spread his hands to grasp the edges of the desk I felt that if he wished he could fold it like a book, clamping his inkpot and papers in the middle. When he spoke his thin lips barely opened. He might have had no teeth at all.

"Well, Mr. Denham," he said, in a voice which twanged like a banjo wire, "take a chair. I'm glad you've come around."

He rose and took my hand, not removing his eyes from mine for a moment. Had I had something on my conscience they would have sucked the sweat out of my brow. "Well," he said after a slight pause, putting himself across from me at his desk under the blue rows of reports, "what can I do for you?"

I told him I had called merely from a desire to hear as nearly first-hand as I could what had happened at Yellowhead Lake.

"I might have guessed as much," he replied, tilting back his head, "you are not the first. The newspapers. Wires from the east. Indeed I find it difficult to understand the interest. The case . . . simple enough in its way."

"I was out there, you see," I said. "I returned only a few days ago."

"Of course, that's so. I remember now. . . . It was mentioned to me. I would have made it a point. . . . tell me, Mr. Denham," he asked suddenly, "what do you know about this man Dobble?"

I explained.

"Odd," he said; "I can't place the man. Never forget a face. My job is to remember faces. Yet his name is familiar enough."

"Oh, he's made quite a shout about himself," I replied.

"He's in Jasper now," Wiggins went on, meditatively stirring his fingers through the papers on his desk. "Required a lot of attention. A doctor. Wired for a special nurse from here. Sergeant Flaherty from out there – received his report the other day. Says it's partly nervous shock, he thinks. Still at that the man was badly hurt. Ribs broken, and has had to be treated for cuts on his head and face; a slight concussion. He was knocked completely out. His men found him under some bushes by the lake shore. Flaherty's idea he was hidden there for dead by Tay John and this Spanish woman. I'm not so sure."

"Not Spanish," I corrected.

"Well, foreign anyway. These foreign women are always making trouble."

"Why blame the woman?" I asked. "Dobble was drunk as a lord."

"Perhaps. Still he claims they assaulted him. That's the exact word Flaherty says he used. 'Assaulted.'"

Dobble, it appeared, entering Ardith Aeriola's tent after I had met him on the road, had been sufficiently drunk or sufficiently belligerent to tell Tay John to get back across the lake to his tepee where he belonged. There had been a fight. It couldn't have been "terrific" or prolonged. It was too unequal for that. Tay John threw him against the board walls his own men had made, and then apparently hammered him on the head with a piece of firewood. Afterwards he had carried him outside, laid him under a bush, and went across the lake to round up three of his horses in the dark. He and Ardith rode off into the mountains, believing in the excitement of the moment that Dobble was dead or that, at any rate, if not, he would set the police on them.

"Of course," Wiggins continued, "the woman may have invited Dobble over."

"I don't think so," I interrupted, "not after what happened. In fact, I know she didn't."

"Still she's a bit of a tart," Wiggins replied, "and anyway what I've just told you Flaherty got from her maid. Prejudiced, probably. Dobble is thoroughly incoherent. We're holding the maid for a while to see what happens. She's the only witness. May need her."

"What for?"

"Well, if Dobble signs a complaint. That's what he was going to do at first. Now, according to Flaherty, he seems to feel differently about it. Says he doesn't want a scandal. Must consider his position, whatever that is."

Wiggins rubbed the palm of his hand over the rasp of his close-cropped hair in a gesture of dismissal. "Always the same thing," he said, "a woman like that goes through life creating again the situations she once escaped from. I've found out that she was involved in some sort of a nasty business in New York. Exonerated, of course. Too good looking – likely has a pair of legs. No matter. She draws men like a piece of bad meat draws flies. And now she's out in the mountains with this half-breed trapper. Now, how long do you think that'll last till we'll have to send someone out after them on some fool report or other? Why do you think she went out in the first place?"

"Perhaps," I said, "perhaps to get away from these very situations you talk about. She may be tired of being followed about."

"Yes, but a half-breed fellow with yellow hair . . ."

"Perhaps as good a man as she's met," I retorted.

"Well, I'll tell you, Mr. Denham." Wiggins rising from his chair put himself back on his heels, lifted his head until he seemed to be addressing the ceiling. He had small pink ears set very high, and as he talked they flushed red. "I know a thing or two about such women," he said. "She won't be able to stick it. A trapper's cabin in dead of winter – if he has a cabin. We'll find her by the railroad track one morning, if we're lucky, looking for a train east. If not . . . if not . . . you mark my words, there'll be something come out of it. We'll hear something, and we'll have to go and investigate. The whole thing isn't logical," he concluded.

What logic there was, I thought as I left Wiggins' office, would not be ours. Each of them, Ardith and Tay John, in manners distinct, stalked the boundaries of society without every fully entering. They had that in common. They had in common, too, the obedience to impulse, seizing the precarious promise of the moment as a trout will seize a fly, opposed to the rest of us whose security is the measure of our denials. I reasoned – she hadn't fled from Dobble, or from fear of retribution because of Dobble, so much as she had fled from the life whose image he was, the life whose humiliations paid for its necessities. Tay John, her guide, was at her side, a man no better nor worse than the others, but different. I have no doubt that, in the only way she could, she had assured herself of his need.

As for Dobble. Later that autumn, following his return to Lucerne from Jasper, he left for the east. He did not come back. His men were paid off by the bank, which had a lien on his holdings. The buildings stayed there for months, their roofs sagging under the snow. They fell into disuse. Trappers, trainmen, and others filched the logs for needs in other places. The cabins disappeared bit by bit, one by one, as though slowly sinking into the ground. You might say that Dobble left barely a trace behind him. Perhaps his investments in the East had gone bad. The name Lucerne caught on. The railway was looking for names. For a long time the sign-post he had erected stood by the track.

The next summer, an unusual thing for me, I was in town. Even more unusual, I accepted an invitation to a tea-party – a standing invitation. Tea-party invitations are always that. It was in honour of some visiting member of the British Parliament – a Tory, I believe. Perhaps one of those fellows who held that life should be an exercise of charity towards the rich, and that the rights of small countries should be protected so long as such protection is not needed. At any rate, we did not meet, which assured the dullness of the party, an end to which all of us strove most successfully.

It took place in a big house with a view over the Saskatchewan. I stood by the window looking down on the river. Nothing like having a river at your tea-party. Jay Wiggins, whom I had not met since my visit to his office, came up to me.

"Well, Mr. Denham, I've got some news for you," he said.

"What . . . a place in your jail?"

"No, no. Nothing so drastic as that . . . not yet, at any rate." He fastened me with his unmoving half-lidded eye. I thought it had a hopeful gleam.

"I refer to your yellow-haired Indian friend and his . . . his consort. You see, one of my men met them, in the foothills west of the Smokey. They were the ones all right – there's no mistaking a pair like that. Yes – we cover the country. It's our assignment. We know its fevers, its chills, its nervous shocks, as a physician knows his patient. Sergeant Flaherty of Jasper met them. They were alone, travelling west into the mountains. He stopped by their tepee. It was a fine site, he said, on a point in the river. This yellow-haired fellow . . . what's his name again?"

"Tay John," I said.

"Of course, Tay John. Well, Tay John and this Spanish woman . . ."

Ardith Aeriola was not Spanish. Central European, I reminded him – not that it, after all, was of importance.

"Well, well, whatever she is. She had a silver cross at her throat anyway." Wiggins brushed my remark aside. He went on to say that Flaherty, naturally enough, and as was in its way his duty, asked Tay John where they were travelling, or if they were travelling at all. He had heard the tinkle of a horse-bell in the timber and seen unshod hoof-marks at a creek crossing.

Tay John made a motion with his arm, the one with the hook on it, towards the mountains. They were going far into the mountains, he said.

Flaherty ate with them. Ardith Aeriola had baked a cut of caribou in the ground. The meat was out of season. Flaherty winked his eye at that – for Tay John, while he would not be granted the freedom of the Indian in his hunting, not being with a recognised band, could hardly be bound to the restrictions of the white man. He had to live, was how Flaherty saw it.

Ardith wore a buckskin jacket and trousers, as ill-made and crudely fitting as if they had been cut for another. She was burnt almost black by the sun, her hair in two long plaits down her back. Throughout the meal Flaherty had been unable to meet her eyes – those dark eyes rimmed with blue-tinged and translucent white. She hid them from him, fearful of what they would reveal.

He said something to her of missing the life she had known. He wondered if before the winter they would be coming back. She knew he meant to the railway, to town, to people, to music, to her own kind. When he had spoken he bit his tongue, for Tay John rose up and walked away.

Ardith and Flaherty rose with him. Ardith took a few steps towards the river. She turned slowly. She traced a circle with a neat moccasined foot through the grass. She looked at Flaherty, chin up – a chin which was none too steady.

"You tell them," she said, as if hundreds of people hung upon her words, "you tell them I'm not going back . . . ever."

Yet Flaherty felt when he was in the saddle that if he had held his hand down to her, she would have mounted and ridden off behind him on his horse's rump. It would have been possible, too, he said, because Tay John had vanished up the river. They were alone. Perhaps later Flaherty came to regret his denial of a romantic mission – Flaherty, a wide, full man in his fifties, a startled face, a ragged moustache suggesting a small furred creature struggling in his mouth.

However he did not offer her his hand. She gave to him the halter shank of his pack pony. Flaherty rode away. She stood on a knoll, eyes squinting against the sun, wind frisking the fringes of her jacket. From the bend of the trail, he looked back. She waved a brown hand. From farther down he looked back again. She was still there, hand upraised, sun catching the silver cross at her throat. Behind her was the smoking tepee. Behind it the wooded hills, and beyond the hills the great blue wall of the Rockies.

"You see," Wiggins explained, "perhaps I was wrong. They seem to have made some sort of an adjustment, the two of them. A working agreement. Only one thing worries me a bit. Flaherty told me – he was in town only a few days ago – that he thought, only thought, mind you, the woman was pregnant."

"Pregnant! Up in that country?"

"Indeed." For the first time Wiggins smiled. For the first time I saw keen, white teeth beneath his clip of a moustache. "It can happen almost anywhere, Mr. Denham – except, perhaps, in solitary confinement. And Flaherty, of course, might have been mistaken. He is a married man – probably not quite so apt in the diagnosis as bachelors such as you and I. According to Flaherty she didn't stand. She seemed about to tip. She was tilted on the little knoll against the far-off mountains.

"Don't worry," he said to me in leaving, as though I had a personal concern in the outcome, "your yellow-haired friend will probably get her down somewhere to be looked after."

That might have been the last I would have heard of Tay John and Ardith Aeriola, but it must be that my fancies were too well caught in the snarls of their destiny. Six months – maybe a year, or two years – after Wiggins had spoken to me, a trapper came "outside" – a good word that, to denote the man's experience of leaving the shelter of the world he knows, of forest and muskeg and river, for the brief and treacherous period in town, with money from furs sold in his pocket and hunger for food, liquor, and company in his body. He came from the country beyond the head of the Jackpine. Wild country. A very mother of rivers – a mountain – still unnamed, is there. Many small streams begin upon its snow- and ice-covered slopes, born to great destinies, to swell the waters of the Peace, and so on into the Slave and Mackenzie which pays lordly tribute to the Arctic. To the west the Pacific, through the far-reaching watershed of the Fraser, takes its toll.

This trapper's name was Blackie – just that, no more. Somewhere in there, more than a hundred miles back from the railway, he had a cabin. He was a great traveller, versed in the ritual and suffering of travel – man's form of worship of the vast round earth. Thirty miles of trail-breaking a day, ninety pounds upon his back, was routine work for Blackie. Years of practice on snowshoes had given him a shambling gait, so that even here in town he walked with his feet wide spaced, the soles of his boots barely clearing the pavement on which he walked.

His body rolled on its hips like a sailor's. His shoulders seemed bent with the weight of his ponderous hands, held not at his side, but in front of him, his arms stiff and not swinging to his gait. He was a big man, over six-foot tall, and his chest, not so broad as it was deep, gave to his voice a resounding quality, like a voice out of a cave. He had the black-bearded face, brown gleaming eyes deep in under his shaggy eyebrows, the dark brow of a prophet. Like a prophet, too, he spoke in amazement of where he had been, of what he had seen, of the things he had heard. Albino bears, hybrid creatures born of the union of a moose and caribou, a pack of wolves led by a collie-dog gone wild, wolverines that could outwit a man — tales such as those Blackie garnered with his furs. Yet immediately upon his arrival in the city he took from their case a pair of gold-rimmed spectacles as if fearful that his eyes alone could not be trusted to deliver a faithful report of what they saw about him.

Up there in that north country, on his way out to the railway, his furs upon his back, he had met Tay John and Ardith Aeriola. "A tall fellow," Blackie said, not knowing his name, "brown in the face like an Indian. An Indian-like sort of fellow, except he had yellow hair. He had only one hand, too. He had a sort of harness business on his shoulders. He was pulling a toboggan."

They met on the middle of a lake in a blizzard. It was not a large lake, but the snow flew so fast and thick that Blackie when he looked around couldn't see the trees along the shore nor beyond them the mountains. "Might as well ha' been on the prairie," was the way Blackie put it. "It was half-dark like night, what with the wind blowin' and the noise of it in my ears."

They were close together before each saw the other. Blackie stopped. Tay John came on, more distinct now, through the curtain of swirling snow, entangled in it, wrapped in its folds, his figure appearing close, then falling back into the mists, a shoulder, a leg, a snowshoe moving on as it were of its own accord – like something spawned by the mists striving to take form before mortal eyes.

"He seemed very big off there, shadowy like," Blackie said, "then again no bigger than a little boy. Then he was standin' in front of me and talkin'. It was hard to see him with the snow, an' hard to hear him with the wind. But he was lean – very lean. I never seen a man standing up so lean. He moved in the wind like he was to fall. His eyes had a hungry look in 'em. He looked fierce and starved, with that yellow hair blowin' across his face. Behind him he had a big load tied on that toboggan, but I didn't see what it was. He got between me and it.

"Then he asked me sudden where was a doctor. Christ, I didn't know! There was no doctor around for a hundred miles, maybe more. I didn't know. I told him. I told him he was heading the wrong way, anyway. He didn't seem to know where he was goin', or to care much, for that matter.

"Then," Blackie went on, "he sort o' caved-in in the middle, like he had a cramp. He had been travelin' pretty hard, I guess. Then he looked up. He had forgotten all about the doctor. He said to me, not askin' questions this time, but telling me: 'I'm going to a church. There's a church over there behind the mountain.' That's what he said. The man was so done in he was havin' visions – or else he was just plain crazy. A church! . . . An' we couldn't even see the mountain, with the snow and the wind howlin'."

There were the two of them in the middle of that God-forsaken lake, talking about churches. Of course Ardith, a Catholic, would have thought of a church. She would have thought of a church and a priest and the peace of holy ground. She would have wanted that.

Tay John went on, leaving Blackie to stare after him. As the toboggan passed, Blackie saw someone tied with ropes on to it. A woman wrapped in a blanket. Her black hair was loose and hung down past her shoulders. She was sitting up, her back towards Tay John. One eye was open. The other closed. "It was like she winked at me," Blackie said. "Her mouth was open, too, just a little, enough so that I thought perhaps she said something I didn't hear. Then I saw snow in her mouth. It was chock-full of snow. One of her hands was dragging in the snow by the toboggan. It made a furrow of its own. She was dead. This yellow-headed fellow was pullin' a dead woman on the toboggan behind him. I could feel hair growin' along my backbone – I was sort of sick in the stomach. I never made such fast time as I did gettin' off that lake."

This had happened some time in the afternoon. After a night to think it over, around his camp-fire underneath a spruce-tree, Blackie decided he had better leave his pack and back-track to see what he could do to help. He explained he couldn't go away and leave a man wandering through the mountains, looking for a church where there was no church within a week's travel, and a dead woman on a toboggan to face him every time he stopped. No, Blackie felt he had to do something.

In the morning he crossed the lake again and found Tay John's sled tracks pretty well snowed over where he had entered the timber. He followed the trail in and out among the trees. It made in one place a wide circle and returned to within a hundred yards of where it had been before. "The man was all in," Blackie said; "he didn't know where he was goin'. He stumbled. I saw where he fell, and had to pull himself up by the branches of a tree."

Tay John had gone on, climbing slowly up the valley until he was beyond the timber. Up there the snow flew faster. His trail became difficult to follow. The valley forked. Blackie looked up into two passes. He didn't know which one Tay John had taken.

It was dusk by then. Cold. A tree cracked. Blackie's breath hissed, rose yellow as grass smoke before his eyes. There was no wind. The snow fell in great wavering flakes without cessation, as if it would go on snowing for ever, as if all the clouds had been upended. The trees, the mountains, the ice on the rivers, all the familiar world, the sky itself were gone from sight.

Blackie stared at the tracks in front of him, very faint now, a slight trough in the snow, no more. Always deeper and deeper into the snow. He turned back then. There was nothing more he could do. He had the feeling, he said, looking down at the tracks, that Tay John hadn't gone over the pass at all. He had just walked down, the toboggan behind him, under the snow and into the ground.

AFTERWORD

BY MICHAEL ONDAATJE

Howard O'Hagan's *Tay John* was one of the first novels to chart important motifs that have become crucial to the work of later western writers like Robert Kroetsch and Rudy Wiebe. O'Hagan's mythic realism seems to me, in fact, much more apt as a way of portraying the west and much of this country than magic realism, which doesn't really seem to nestle that convincingly with the cold-blooded sternness that is at the heart of the Canadian character. O'Hagan charts a clash of romance and myth against the cold realities of a progress-oriented world.

O'Hagan doesn't just sweep the plot along. He darts about, in that outrider's movement, trying to shape and make something as clearly and energetically as he can. The novel as sculpture. The novel as wagon-train. So we can walk around it, ride back, and find hidden caves and clues that lead back to Chapter One. This is not just a race to the end of the novel to find out who will win. There is a pleasure of architecture, a pleasure of choreography.

O'Hagan stepped away from his careers as a mountain guide in the British Columbia interior and then as a railway man in South America to bring to our literature a voice from the real world. In his other writings, he teaches us how to track a wolverine or how to live off the country without perverting it with names or social laws. He brings with him a dark and scornful sense of irony toward civilization. "Vanity, vanity . . . the fat upon the spirit." One always has a sense that O'Hagan and his narrators are from a leaner, silent world. They circle us with their stories and trap us with terrific yarns which are operatic from having been composed in too much solitude.

The fashion in our generation is to have stories of heroes told by anti-heroes. Narrators have forced themselves – along with their inhibitions and qualitative judgments – on to the original source of the story until their books have become psychological studies or witty and ironic monologues. Vladimir Nabokov's *Pale Fire* and Robert Kroetsch's *The Studhorse Man* are two satirical examples of how narrators insist on making themselves the heroes in someone else's tale. The hero has been qualified or masked to death, and we have to go back to Joseph Conrad to find a moderate and humane balance between story-teller and central character. Yet even Conrad's compassion and identification suggest a great weakening in the status of the hero. The power of Greek tragedy was, after all, caused by the very fact that the narrators, or Chorus, had no true understanding of the dogmatic, determined power of the central character.

It is not often that one finds a book in which the original myth is given to us point-blank. These days, writing may be finer, more careful, more witty, but it has lost that original rawness. Few novels get as close to such raw power as *Tay John* does. The hero's tale is left intact, and the source of the legend is never qualified.

The story remains potent because of the way O'Hagan has found a legend and retold it in the form of a myth. The cast is small. Narrators are recognized as minor characters. The mysterious centre is given power to grow. O'Hagan, one senses, understands where the dramatic sources of myth lie. There are three or four scenes that take up not much more than an eighth of the novel but whose strength invades the rest of the book.

Myth is also created by a very careful use of echoes – of phrases and images. There may be no logical connection when these are placed side by side, but the variations are always there setting up parallels. Tay John chops off his hand; the woman Ardith cuts off the nails of a baby bear to stop it scratching her, and the paws bleed. Tay John chases an escaped horse and is seen with some of the hairs from its tail in his hand; after a fight from which Tay John escapes, one of the men finds some yellow hair in his fingers.

The use of echoes is crucial to the myth for the action in the novel turns in on itself, is incestuous. O'Hagan is aware that legend needs only two or three images to sustain it; myth breeds on itself no matter what the situation or landscape. This is especially important here, for the landscape is being changed with the oncoming railroad; the fragments and formulas of myth, however, will repeat themselves forever.

The most consistent and carefully plotted image is Tay John's birth from and eventual disappearance into the earth. This link of Tay John and earth physically parallels the strange and dark asides of the narrator, Jack Denham, in a crucial way. Tay John is little more than seasonal grass. He *has* to disappear. From the very beginning he is a part of nature, and this fateful metaphor will also assure his rebirth. As his mother was buried pregnant, so he goes into the snow at the end with his dead and pregnant woman. And the pulling of the toboggan that carries her reminds us subconsciously of an earlier passage which speaks of man's shadow.

> Men walk upon the earth in light, trailing their shadows that are the day's memories of the night. For each man his shadow is his dark garment . . . it is his shroud, awaiting him by his mother's womb lest he forget what, with his first breath of life, he no longer remembers.

Denham's asides represent partly the voice of Indian legends but also the world view of O'Hagan. They unify the book by being the mediation between the physical glimpses of the raw myth. They are a comical vision of the world – Jack Denham sees all civilization as ephemeral and tragic for those who take their foothold on the earth too seriously.

> To-day was implicit in time's beginning. And all that is, was. Somewhere light glowed in the first vast and awful darkness, and darkness is the hub of light. Imprisoned in its fires which brighten and make visible the universe, and shine upon man's face, is the core, the centre, the hard unity of the sun, and it is dark.

The witnessing of the arrival and disappearance of a myth and Tay John's fragility in the midst of civilization must be seen in this context. Man is a pulse of light in a dark landscape. He disappears into historical time and re-emerges in an echo. The civilization growing up around Tay John is ludicrous in its self-importance. In the midst of its birth it feels no need to destroy him – it doesn't have to. The book contains no obvious myth of the scapegoat removed from society. Everything will disappear. Dobble's dream of a "Lucerne in the

Rockies" in the end rots under the snow. "You might say that Dobble left barely a trace behind him."

Once O'Hagan establishes the base of the book – the myth with its power and its fragility – he is able to turn to the role of story-tellers. These men are separate from the source of power. They may eat off the table that has soaked up Tay John's blood but they get no closer. In the superb scene in which Tay John fights the bear, Jack Denham, who witnesses it, is separated by a raging river he cannot cross but which is only two yards wide. He is unable to cross over into the arena of pure myth. And not till the fight is over does Denham provide a social context. "He had won. *We* had won. That was how I felt. I shouted. I did a dance. . . . A victory is no victory until it has been shared."

And so the event becomes the centre of "Jackie's tale," told to his cronies in the bars Denham inhabits, and for the rest of the book it is Denham who searches for "the remnants of his presence." Denham, we discover, is one of those men who love the wilderness as opposed to "the treacherous period in town" but who are still overcome by raw nature:

> when you turn your back upon it you feel that it may drop back again into the dusk that gave it being. It is only your vision that holds it in the known and created world. It is physically exhausting to look on unnamed country. A name is the magic to keep it within the horizons. Put a name to it, put it on a map, and you've got it. The unnamed – it is the darkness unveiled.

If there is irony and qualification in the novel, it is directed not toward the source of the myth but toward the story-teller's need for order. Tay John comes into the world without a name or shadow, and he is given several names and several kinds of shadows "to align him with the human race." But words are part of the imperialistic disguise for an unnamed country. Words bring morality and immorality. Tay John himself says hardly more than two sentences in the whole book. The action of the novel begins when Red Rorty the trapper takes the words of a preacher literally: "We who believe . . . are a small army. We must go out and take our message to all the world."

Most revealing on the status of the word is Rorty's death when he is tied to a tree and his beard set on fire. "They found the skull, fallen to the ground and caught in the black twisted roots of a tree. The stone was still between its jaws. Yaada took a stick and pointed. 'See!' she said, 'he was a great liar, and the word has choked him!'"

Religion, like the word, brings values that are totally unnatural to the landscape, and it takes men such as Father Rorty with his "priestly arrogance" down twisted, guilty paths to suicide. Even Tay John in his hand-chopping scene echoes his father's naive belief in words and metaphors and performs the act yelling, "If your hand offend you – cut it off." It is his one unnatural act. The Shuswap tribe is also riddled with customs and words and, although they are "closer neighbours" to the earth, Tay John leaves them when their ceremonies and laws limit him. They too are waiting for the moral voice of a leader.

As a narrator Denham is saved by his neutrality, his interest in other events. He has his own life to live. He is not, like Conrad's Marlow, living almost by proxy. And he knows the story will exist without him.

> Not that I feel any responsibility to Tay John, nor to his
> story. No, not at all. His story, such as it is, like himself,

would have existed independently of me . . . every story only waits, like a mountain in an untravelled land, for someone to come close, to gaze upon its contours, lay a name upon it, and relate it to the known world. Indeed, to tell a story is to leave most of it untold.

Denham, then, is not the secure, more assured narrator of Conrad's Europe, but a voice genuinely apt for describing an unfinished legend that is shaping itself before his eyes. Tay John's life is seen only in the brief seconds of lightning in the night; the rest is tentative meditation. The source, therefore, dominates our minds.

For these reasons the style of the book and its themes are sensitively linked. There is, for instance, a very specific way in which O'Hagan describes his characters, and this structure of characterization parallels the movement of the whole book: Take the first descriptions of Red Rorty that deal with him as a fragment of the landscape: "In 1880 one man remained by the Athabaska river where it flowed through the mountains." Then we are given one detail about Rorty – his ability to shout. The paragraph ends by moving from this clear image into something that is almost mystical:

At other times he would shout when there was nothing to shout for, and would listen and smile when the mountains hurled his voice – rolled it from one rock wall to another, until it seemed he heard bands of men, loosed above him, calling one to another as they climbed farther and higher into the rock and ice.

The long shot, then the close-up, then the eventual dissolving out of focus into something mysterious and inchoate is the general movement of the whole book. After the tough, tight power of the first two sections, the last section is diffuse and scattered – literally "Evidence – without a finding." This has an irritating effect on the reader. For instance, where the book should be reaching its crisis or denouement, four pages from the end, O'Hagan suddenly introduces a new character-witness, Blackie, and gives us a portrait of him that takes up two of the last four pages. The story is taken away from Tay John. What is important about legends now is the effect they have on other men. And, as with all stories told, it is crucial for us to trust and believe in the character of the story-teller.

Both Tay John and Ardith, though hero and heroine, have lived on the boundaries of civilizations. Tay John is the accidental intruder in every scene – in the world of the Shuswaps, with the Aldersons, in the resort at "Lucerne." He is given new names in every setting and he slides through all his roles like water. He leaves only fragments of his myth behind; he has no cause or motive or moral to announce, and as a result is of no worth in the new societies of commerce, religion, and imperialism. His life, in the midst of all the words, is wordless – as the core of the sun, which gives off so much light, is pitch black. He is vulnerable to fashion and progress and his only strength is the grain left in the memory and in the hope he will emerge in the future in different forms.

Any reader or writer likes to find his own literary touchstones. These are often books that are not part of the great tradition. They are more like outriders – books that burn or splash on the periphery. These works enter us not as part of a curriculum but as the markings on a personal map to which we know, subconsciously, we belong.

The first Canadian novel to reach me this way was Sheila Watson's *The Double Hook*. The second was *Tay John*. To come later were *By Grand Central Station I Sat Down and Wept* by Elizabeth Smart and *Swamp Angel* by Ethel Wilson. Seen together they are, in a way, a tradition. *Tay John* in 1939, *By Grand Central Station I Sat Down and Wept* in 1945, *Swamp Angel* in 1954, *The Double Hook* in 1959: the beginnings of the contemporary novel in Canada. It is an uncomfortable tradition, but for me these writers are to be loved because of the kind of books they wrote – private and eternal, gnarled and graceful, regional and mythical.

The four books are not part of the realistic tradition that seems to continue endlessly and without wit. The authors of these books are selective, as a good guide in a wilderness should be. They know we do not need to be given the whole history of the place. They have a succinctness and they have a roving narrative voice and eye that allow them to come at the story from many angles. When a reader gets such abrupt shifts and quick swerves, he finds himself in a map of metaphors and has to explore the connections on his own. No lecturing or finger pointing goes on here, at least not without a sense of irony. All of these books have double-barrelled or double-hooked points of view.

These novels also share a sense of geography that results in a deep connectedness between the characters and place. There is this line from *Swamp Angel*: "She also developed a jealousy against the lake as against a person." In these works the landscape moves around as in no other novel, *behaving* towards characters. It is not a landscape that just sits back and damns the characters with droughts. It is quicksilver, changeable, human – and we are no longer part of the realistic novel, and no longer part of the European tradition.

BY HOWARD O'HAGAN

BIOGRAPHY

Wilderness Men (1958)

FICTION

Tay John (1939)

The Woman Who Got on at Jasper Station and
Other Stories (1963)

The School Marm Tree (1977)